FALSE HORIZON

FALSE HORIZON

BOOK ONE OF THE OLINC MIRAGE

IRA RUSSELL

This is a work of fiction. Names, characters, places, and incidents are either products of the author's imagination or are used fictitiously. Any resemblance to actual persons, living or dead, businesses, companies, events, or locales is entirely coincidental.

Paperback ISBN: 978-1-950741-19-9

Cover design by Inky's Nest Design Group

Edited by Jennifer Lovell

Published by Inky's Nest Publishing

Printed in the United States of America

For those who look at the horizon and dare to ask if the shimmering they see is the heat, or the Truth.

ONE

The guy sitting directly across from me in the holding cell worried me the most. It wasn't his unkempt blond hair or the way he would mumble to himself that bothered me so much. It was the way he watched me incessantly. Worst of all, whenever I would glance his way, there was something deeply unnerving about the way he wouldn't break his gaze. Most people would turn away when they were caught staring at someone, but not him.

Periodically, the left side of his lips would curl up into the tiniest bit of a smile. I couldn't help but assume he thought he understood something about me that nobody else knew, including me.

He didn't know anything about me, though. Nothing. Nobody in here did. They probably all figured I was just another criminal, but I had never so much as stolen a stick of gum or sneaked into a movie theater. I didn't belong in here. I had just been in the wrong place at the wrong time. This was all Jason's fault.

I looked over at Jason again, who just shrugged his shoulders as if to say, "These things happen." He was sitting next to a man who had both his feet up on the bench and his arms around his knees. The man was clearly in agony, and it was easy to assume he was painfully withdrawing from some sort of drug.

As I was sitting there frustrated with Jason's indifferent attitude toward all of this, I heard the blond guy say something under his breath.

It was barely audible, but when I turned my eyes back toward him, he spoke again, much louder this time. "What are you doing in here?" he asked through gritted teeth.

I jumped a little in my seat. He was making his way over to me with those penetrating eyes. He was close enough now that I could see they were an unusually light shade of piercing green.

"What ... are you ... doing here?" he repeated, more forcefully this time.

"I—" I didn't know how to respond because I didn't know quite what type of answer he was hunting for.

"You don't belong here. You're not one of us," he said, pointing a shaking finger directly into my face. "You're up to something."

I still didn't know what to say. Up until that moment, although I was completely out of my element, I didn't realize how much my outer appearance matched the way I felt inside.

"It won't work. Not on me." He turned his head slightly away but kept his eyes glued to mine as he stepped back to his spot on the bench directly across the room from me. "You can't fool me. Nope. I'm no fool."

I kept part of my attention fixed on him as the door opened and three figures stepped in. The first was the same man I had seen all day, dressed in his guard uniform and holding a set of keys in one hand.

Behind him stood a young man and woman, both roughly my age at twenty-five.

The young man was meticulously dressed. He wore a tailored navy-blue suit with pant legs that hovered an inch above a pair of brown leather shoes that looked to be worth more than my pickup truck. When he reached up to straighten his neon-green necktie, his right sleeve pulled back enough to reveal a wristwatch that made his shoes look like those of a pauper.

He was scanning the room like he was shopping, studying each of us and sizing us up in turn as if to decide which one he wanted to wrap up and take home.

When he glanced at me, I couldn't help but think my eyes probably screamed, "Me! Me! Pick me! I have no idea what you want with any of us, but anywhere is better than in here with Mr. Green Eyes over there ready to attack me." But his glance couldn't have lasted longer than maybe a second and a half before he moved on to the next guy. I sighed. He obviously wasn't interested in picking me, so my next hope was that he would select Mr. Green Eyes so I wouldn't have to worry about him anymore.

"What's your name? Why are you in here?" the young man finally said as he walked across the room and stopped one step in front of Jason.

"Jason. I got caught stealing." He shrugged his shoulders in the same way he had been doing every time I made eye contact with him. "What are ya gonna do? Am I right?"

The young man folded his arms and stared. He stood there studying Jason for so long that even Jason began to grow uncomfortable and started looking around the room at anything except the man standing over him.

"Okay. This guy," the young man said before turning on his heel and walking away, back toward the girl.

"Me? What do you want with me?" Jason asked, obviously a bit worried.

He brushed past the guard and was about to pass the young lady when she finally spoke up.

"I'd like to talk to him," she said, looking directly at me. She didn't point a finger or step any closer, but it was obvious to everyone in the room that I was the one she was referring to.

"Why?" the young man asked. "He's boring."

I was surprised a bit when she rolled her eyes at his words. That minute gesture, as well as her physical appearance, told me volumes about her and about their relationship. She wore blue jeans and Skechers on her feet. Tucked into those jeans was a white T-shirt of a yellow submarine and the four faces of the Beatles above it. She clearly was not as worried as her partner about being flashy, and yet, she was stunningly beautiful. Her type of beauty was natural—the kind that would not be extinguished by a bad hair day or by catching her without makeup.

When she had rolled her eyes, all at once she had conveyed the fact that she was not as impressed by him as he wanted everyone to be, and his lack of surprise at the gesture made it easy to see he had given up on that hope long ago.

The young man looked at me for a long moment as if he were waiting for something. Since I didn't know what on earth he was waiting for. I just sat there clueless until he said, "Okay, fine. We can talk to them both."

Jason and I stood in unison. We followed the guard out through the door and down the hall to where a door stood open and the five of us stepped in together. A square white table sat in the middle of the small room with four chairs around it.

"We'll be fine," the young woman said to the guard. "You don't have to worry about us."

With that, the guard vacated the room and the rest of us each selected a chair around the small table.

"My name is Ramsey Mir, and my partner here is Summer Bishop," the young man said. He paused for a moment as if he were allowing us time to absorb that information. He leaned back in his chair, folded his arms, and smiled a large friendly smile.

I was a bit taken aback by the sudden shift in his aura. Up until this point, he seemed to be all business and seriousness. Because of that, my initial reaction was to distrust his smile as if he were some stereotypical salesman trying to sell me a timeshare in Death Valley or something. But he and Summer looked at each other with another glance that told volumes. It was as if their eyes were saying to each other, "Here we go. The ride begins. The moment we've all been waiting so long for."

That made me wonder what all of this could possibly be about. Just an hour and a half ago I had found myself in handcuffs for the first time in my life. Ever since that moment, all I could think about was how to slip out of these charges, but my mind came up blank with every option. I had nothing to offer the system in exchange for mercy. I knew nothing about any real criminals, so I couldn't rat on anyone in exchange for leniency. Whatever type of deal these two were here to offer me, I couldn't think of anything I had to offer in return. But then again, these two did not seem like they were cops, or detectives, or FBI, or CIA, or any other type of official agency my racing mind could conjure up.

"You two can just relax," Ramsey said. "We aren't here to nail you down with anything. We aren't gonna judge you or try to get you to do anything you don't want to do."

"Breaking and entering?" Summer said. She was holding a piece of paper in each hand, looking back and forth at them. "Were you two together at the time? Are you friends?"

Jason and I glanced at each other before Jason said, "We were together, yes."

I knew what he was thinking and why he avoided answering the second half of the question. We weren't really friends. We had been once upon a time—way back in the fifth grade when we both had Mrs. Slonecker for a teacher, but that was many years ago. Friends? No. We weren't friends anymore. Today was the first time we had done anything at all together in more than a decade.

"I don't see it. You don't look like a criminal to me," Summer said, studying me a little more. "But that doesn't matter right now." She placed one paper on top of the other and turned them face down on the table. "We don't care what you've done. You didn't kill someone. You're not gangsters or predators or anything like that. So, we want to offer you an alternative to jail time."

"We want you to be part of an experiment," Ramsey added. "We have created a sort of ... a ... we have created an alternate world, I guess you could say."

"An Artificial Intelligence world," Summer added. "It's the most amazing thing. It will give you an opportunity to live your life more like normal people and prove yourself without having to spend time in an orange jumpsuit. You see, we feel like the community doesn't gain anything at all from locking you guys up. Some people benefit from some time in jail, but I think some people go in as relatively normal people but come out harder than they—"

"You want to stick me in the Matrix," Jason said scoffingly. "You want to hook me up to some machine or put me in a coma or something, and send my brain into the Matrix where I have to go through all kinds of mental obstacle courses to prove myself in some weird, twisted way." He shook his head unbelievingly, looking back and forth between Ramsey and Summer. "You want to stick me in some crazy scenario where I have to help an old lady cross the street when—BAM! Here comes a dragon or something! And then when I successfully get the old lady across the street ... Oh, no. Look out—tornado! Get into the cellar! Uh oh. Then the house collapses and we are stuck. There's not enough food for both of us. I guess I need to prove I'm a good guy by giving Grandma my portion of the food!"

Ramsey made only a slight attempt to hide his amusement. "That's actually a pretty good idea," he said, then turned to Summer. "Let's make sure to add Grandma and a twister as soon as we get back."

"And a dragon, of course." Summer snickered. "Probably better to just give it one head, though. A two-headed dragon would be taking things too far."

"Too far," Ramsey agreed, and the two of them shared a laugh.

"Okay. Okay. You mock me," Jason said. "Then what is it like? What is your precious Matrix like?"

Summer took a deep breath and considered for a moment how to answer his question before responding. "Well, most of what it's like needs to remain a bit of a mystery, I guess you could say. That's part of the experiment. The less you know, the better it is for the experiment."

"The less you know, the better," Ramsey agreed. "The only thing you really need to know right now is that this 'Matrix,' as you like to call it, is very true to normal, everyday life. There are no dragons. There will be no tornadoes."

"Unless a real tornado happens to blow through the town for real, that is," Summer interjected.

Jason threw his hands up in the air in frustration. "Wait, so is it a Matrix or not? Is it an alternative world or not? If a tornado blows through town for real, how is it in the Matrix?"

"We can't really tell you that. You'll just have to trust us," Summer said. "It's hard, I know. But you'll just have to trust us."

"Yeah, well, you've given me nothing to go on. Why would I trust you?" Jason looked at Summer and sneered. "There's nothing special about you. You look like every pretty little young housewife who got married right out of high school and just started popping out perfect little kids. What do you even know about proving yourself in the real world?" He then turned his attention over to Ramsey and looked him up and down. "And you ... I don't even know where to begin with you. The two of you give me no way of understanding what your Matrix is like, and then you mock me as I try to figure it out." He pushed his chair back from the table. "You'll have to forgive me if I don't jump at the chance to trust you enough to turn me into your little lab rat."

"Suit yourself," Ramsey said. "I think you're missing a fun opportunity here, but we aren't going to bend over backward to try to convince you. It's all up to you."

"Got that right. It is all up to me." Jason stood up. He took three steps toward the door before turning back. "And how does one even get into this Matrix of yours anyway? Would you put me into a coma? Plug some extension cord into the back of my brain stem or something?"

"That is actually the biggest part of where you would need to trust us," Summer said. She wasn't looking at Jason when she said it. Even though I hadn't said a single word since we came into the room, her attention was now turned to me. "It's hard to trust a couple of strangers, we know, but there would be a need to install something right here." She lifted up her hair and placed the tip of her index finger behind her left ear at the base of her skull. "I know we keep using the expression 'experiment' because we can't fill you in on too many of the details yet, but just know that we are completely confident in the procedure being safe."

Jason laughed. "You want to put an implant in my brain so I can be in your Matrix world, and you want me to believe it's completely safe?" He took the last few steps to the door and twisted the knob. "If I had a nickel for every time I heard of someone's brain implant malfunctioning, I could buy a watch like Mr. Playboy over there," he said, pointing at Ramsey. "You want to put a chip in my brain just so I can prove myself worthy of being in your AI world. Ha!" He scoffed, and then he pulled open the door to reveal the security guard standing right there in the doorway. "I think I'll just do my time the normal way, thank you very much."

The guard pulled the door shut behind Jason and the three of us sat silent in the moment. Jason didn't say anything I hadn't been thinking ... except maybe the dragon part, I guess. This whole scenario was crazy. Insane. I would have to be nuts to even consider something like this.

But there was something in Summer's eyes that told me I could trust her. I couldn't quite say the same thing about Ramsey. The jury was still out about him, but I couldn't help but lean my decision on the cues Summer was giving me. I didn't think she had a malicious bone in her body. I didn't think she even had it in her to treat another human being like little more than a "lab rat," even though I clearly would be part of an experiment where she, and possibly a whole bunch of other people, would be monitoring every move I made and probably taking copious notes on their little clipboards or something. I liked to think my trust had more to do with her than my fear of being thrown back into the dungeon with crazy Mr. Green Eyes ready to strangle me in my sleep.

"Look," Ramsey said. "If you don't want to do this, no hard feelings. We can always find someone else who—"

"I think I'm in," I said, cutting him off. "I just want to talk to an attorney first. Is that okay?"

TWO

I was escorted down the hall into one of the secluded rooms where I could chat with my attorney. The guard asked me to have a seat. After I sat, he asked me to lift my hands onto the table before he connected my handcuffs to a metal ring at the center of the table.

This was my first time ever needing to talk to a lawyer, but I knew enough from watching television and reading stories on the internet to know that I wouldn't be talking to a real person. My "attorney" would be an AI personality that I could chat with. I was a bit old-fashioned and hated conversing with AI no matter how well-programmed they were, so I would usually prefer talking to a real person.

That wasn't the case today, though. If I were to request the services of an actual human being with a pulse, I would be tossed right back into the jail with crazy Mr. Green Eyes for at least a few more days before I ever saw that lawyer. Not only that, but today I was mostly interested in information. I was seriously considering the idea of taking these two up on their offer, but I wanted a chance to do a background check on them first. A human lawyer obviously wouldn't have that option built into their brain.

"First of all, I want you to tell me how much jail time I'm looking at here," I said to the image on the television screen in front of me.

"My understanding is that you are being charged with felony burglary," the thing said. "If you are convicted, you are looking at a sentence of somewhere between two and seven years."

"Ouch! Well, let me tell you the whole story and you can tell me if that charge is going to stick," I said, and then I went on to tell him all the details of my day.

"You are not going to get much sympathy with that story," it said.

"What do you even know about sympathy? You're nothing but an algorithm. Don't feed me your nonsense about sympathy."

"Suit yourself," it said, "but I have a lot more experience in these matters than you do. Nobody is going to believe your story."

I folded my arms on top of the table and dropped my face down into my forearms. This was why I hated AI personalities. They looked real enough when I spoke to them on screen, or while wearing a pair of vision glasses, but their realism only made them seem snippy or heartless when trying to talk to them. This thing couldn't care less about whether or not I got off, or got a light sentence, or got the death penalty because this thing didn't have feelings.

So, why then was I even considering the possibility of letting Summer and Ramsey throw me into their AI world? It was easy to assume their invention was going to be just a newer version of this same type of thing. They would probably make me sit in front of an AI therapist for twenty hours a week and pretend I cared what advice the thing was feeding me. That sounded like torture to me. Then again, I doubted crazy Mr. Green Eyes was the only lunatic who would be locked up along with me. Whether I ended up spending all my time in the county jail, or if I were to end up in the prison, surely there would be a lot of people who could make my life a whole lot worse than a non-human therapist trying to interpret my dreams or something.

"I need you to search the net for me," I said. "What can you tell me about Summer Bishop and Ramsey Mir?"

The image on the screen said nothing in response. I waited for a good ten seconds or so before asking if it heard me.

"I heard you," it said. "I'm still searching. Oh, wait, here is something: It looks like Summer Bishop married someone named Logan."

"That's it? Is that all you can tell me? Don't you have access to all the normal data?"

"I do. There is just not much to find."

"Okay, then do a search about me," I said. "Tell me what you know about me."

Without hesitation, it rambled off a long list of facts, including my birthday, every school I attended as a child, the day I got my driver's license, and all kinds of random things. I interrupted the list while it was talking about my high school grade point average.

"Why is it you could tell me the name, age, and hair color of my second-grade teacher, but you can't tell me anything at all about Summer or Ramsey?" I asked.

"I can't tell you information that is not there."

"How could someone erase all their information from the system? Doesn't that seem shady?"

"I have no information or opinion on that," it said.

I told the AI attorney everything I knew about the experiment Summer and Ramsey wanted me to take part in. I wasn't really all that interested in whatever response it was going to give me. Rather, I just needed to lay out all the details so I could decide for myself. When I asked what it thought about the options before me, I expected it to tell me again that it had no information or opinion on the matter, but it responded with, "The proposition seems very suspect and dangerous to me. I recommend you plead guilty to your crime and just do your time."

"Yeah, well what do you know? You're not me. In fact, you're not even a person," I said. "You're just a creation of what the system wants me to do. Just alert the guard that I'm finished in here." I leaned back in my chair to wait.

When the door opened again, I saw Summer and Ramsey standing behind the guard in the doorway.

"What did you decide?" Summer asked as she peeked over the guard's shoulder.

"I'm going to choose to trust you," I said with a nod. "I guess we will see what your AI experiment is all about."

Summer responded with a large smile, while Ramsey just shrugged his shoulders and said once again, "Okay. Fine. But I'm telling you he looks too boring."

I expected there to be a lot more paperwork than there was. A shorter man in an expensive suit came into the room, and over the course of only about five minutes, he repeated four times the line, "You are agreeing to the terms that you are going into this situation unaware of what scenarios may come your way, and you cannot sue for any psychological trauma."

I was fully aware that agreeing to these terms was a stupid thing for me to do. Surely, I would have gotten a light sentence once the judge heard my story, right? I mean, my previous criminal record was a blank sheet of paper. I wasn't completely confident that Jason would have my back, though, because he had absolutely no integrity, but surely a judge, or even a jury, if it came to that, would be able to see the difference between Jason and me, wouldn't they?

My decision to go along with this crazy scheme really had nothing to do with escaping punishment. There was a reason Ramsey had taken one look at me and deemed me too "boring" to be selected for this experiment.

Ramsey was right, though. I was boring. My whole life was boring. Perhaps not in the same way he was saying I was, but all my friends from high school were getting married, having children, climbing the ladder in their careers, and settling down with their white picket-fenced houses. My life consisted of spending the day with the same bunch of guys on my landscaping crew, going on a lot of first dates with girls, but rarely becoming interested enough to go on a second date, and coming home alone to my third-story apartment at the end of it all to watch reruns of FBI Files.

Ramsey was right. I needed something to add a little spice to my existence. I needed an adventure. I needed to stick my keys into the wall socket of my life and shock myself into feeling something completely new.

As the little fancy-talking lawyer dude had kept repeating that same line about not being able to sue for psychological trauma, I couldn't help but look over his shoulder at Summer as she continued to sit calmly in her chair with her hands folded in her lap. I knew almost nothing about her, but I trusted her. From the light smile that rarely left her lips, to the modest wedding ring on her finger that suggested she would be going home in a few hours to spend a quiet evening with her family, to those eyes that looked like they could never view someone as just a lab rat ... I chose to trust her. Forget Ramsey or the little lawyer dude, Summer was the only one who could have gotten me to put my signature on that line.

I signed.

That signature was all it took to get me out of there. I thought I was going to have to stand in front of a judge to talk over the agreement, but no. As soon as I put that pen to paper, we walked right out of that room and out the door. The uniformed guard didn't even bother to walk us out.

At the same time we exited the front doors, a large van pulled up in front of us. At first, because of its size, I thought it was a shuttle bus, but shuttle buses didn't have dark tinted windows, chrome trim, or fancy wheels like this van had. As large as it was, there were only six seats inside. I slid into one at the back. Like all the other seats in this van, it was made of soft leather and spaced out enough that I could fully recline if I wanted to. This thing felt like a small living room on wheels.

Ramsey climbed into the front seat, but instead of grabbing the steering wheel, he pressed a button and his chair spun to face me. "Car, take us to see Dr. Lu."

"Did you say Dr. Boot?" a voice asked over the speaker system.

"No," Ramsey said, a bit frustrated. "Take us to Dr. Lu at Saint Alphonsus Medical Center."

"Taking you to Saint Alphonsus Medical Center," the car said before we began rolling through the parking lot.

Summer sat in the other front seat close to Ramsey. They both studied me, but their expressions told me they were sizing me up differently. Neither of them spoke a whole lot, which was fine with me because the closer we came to the hospital, the more I began to clam up with nerves.

Once we were inside the building, we were escorted directly to a private room in an empty wing of the hospital. There was no time spent in any waiting room. No paperwork. Not even a little lawyer dude there to ask me once again if I was sure I wanted to go through with this.

There were three doctors and two assistants already standing around an operating table when we arrived. I stepped into the bathroom just long enough to change out of my grubby street clothes and into a hospital gown, and in no time at all I was lying on an operating table ready for who-knows-what.

"Hold up one minute," Summer said. She stepped close to me and placed one hand on my shoulder. "I just want to make sure you're okay with this. If you were only agreeing to this to get out of your charges, that's fine. Your charges are dropped now whether you do this or not."

"Wait. That's not how this works," Ramsey said from across the room. "If he backs out now, he just goes back to jail."

Summer shot him a disapproving look, and Ramsey softened without her having to say a word.

"Fine," he said. "If you back out now ... whatever."

I looked at the two of them, and then around the room. Those who were wearing scrubs and face masks were extremely intimidating, and the tray of blades close to my bed was terrifying to look at, but I had already made up my mind.

"I'm good," I said. "I'm in."

Summer's hand remained on my shoulder as one of the assistants slid a needle into a vein in my left arm. She then connected my tube to a bag of liquid above my head that began to drip, drip, drip.

"You are going to be out for quite a while," a nurse said with wrinkles around her eyes, suggesting there was a smile somewhere behind her yellow mask. "Once you do wake up, you will probably feel disoriented, but only for a very short period of time."

"Will I be here in this same room when I wake up?" I asked.

"No," Summer said. "In fact, you won't even be here in Idaho anymore."

THREE

I remember the anesthesiologist telling me to count backward from one hundred, and I think I made it into the mid-eighties before my sense of time crumbled into nothingness.

When I began to open my eyes again, I could sense that it had been a long time since everything had gone blank. It felt different than waking from a long sleep, though. I was sure it had been at least a few days, if not longer.

"Look who's awake," came a gentle womanly voice from beside me. "Welcome to Lincoln City."

I slowly blinked half a dozen times, opening my eyes widely between each blink. When I could finally focus properly, I saw the woman sitting next to me holding my hand. I didn't know what or who I expected to be waiting for me, but her presence was a nice surprise. She had a very calming presence.

In her seated position, her head was at the same level as mine, so with my face turned toward her, our noses were only about twelve inches apart. She looked like she was somewhere around the age of sixty-five. She wore large colorful hoop earrings, and multiple bracelets to match. Other than that, her appearance was quite natural and plain. She wore no makeup. If she had, it would have looked out of place.

"How long was I asleep?" I noticed my mouth tasted horrible, so I turned my head a little to keep my breath from blowing in her face.

She rubbed the back of my hand with her free hand. "Today is January 26th. You were asleep for six days."

I don't know exactly what I was expecting when I awakened, but it wasn't this. I thought I would at least be in some sort of laboratory, if not right in the middle of an archaic sports coliseum with lions ready to chase me through a maze. But as I looked around the room, it looked like any boring middle-priced hotel room. A rather large television was mounted on the wall above a dresser. A small table sat in the corner with two chairs pulled up to it. A small refrigerator sat in the other corner. Other than that, there really wasn't anything to look at.

"Let me open the blinds for you," she said before letting go of my hand.

Without standing up, she turned and began to glide away from my bedside. It wasn't until that moment that I came to realize the chair she had been sitting in was a wheelchair.

I went to sit up but realized I was tethered to a tube connecting me to a bag of clear liquid above my bed, and I dared not move until I could at least know what was going on.

"I think you're really going to like it here." She grabbed the edge of the curtains and pulled them open, revealing a large glass wall and sliding door that opened to a small balcony.

Trying not to move too suddenly, I sat straight up, wide-eyed in my bed.

"What do you say we get some fresh air in here?" She slid open the door.

I couldn't believe it. Not only had I awakened in the most comfortable bed I had ever experienced, but my room was literally right on the ocean. From my vantage point, I could see that my room was most likely about three stories up and right on the shoreline.

The tide was such that the water's edge was crashing onto the sand only about forty yards away. A layer of fog hovered over the horizon, making it so I could just barely make out the sun through the mist. Since I didn't know if that sun was to the east or to the west, I didn't know if it was soon to set, or if it had just come up.

"What country am I in? What ocean is that?" I asked.

"Country?" She laughed. "Oh, honey, you're not all that far away from home. You're still in the United States. This is Oregon. Lincoln City."

"It's so beautiful." I felt like such a fool as the words came out of my mouth. Of course it was beautiful. Of course the picture painted in front of me was one of the most amazing landscapes on the planet. None of it was real. This was the Matrix world they had been talking about back at the police station in Idaho. For all I knew, my real body could be lying flat on some laboratory table somewhere while my mind was right here on the beach.

The lady wheeled herself back to my bedside. "Do you want me to take that thing out of you?" she asked, pointing down at my arm. "I mean, it doesn't look very comfortable, and I'm pretty sure you don't need that anymore."

"Pretty sure?" I asked.

"I'm sure." She smiled. "Or you could pull it out yourself. I mean, I'm not a nurse or anything either."

I looked down at the needle and tube protruding from my arm. I held my arm out to her and closed my eyes. I wasn't scared of her removing the needle, and I wouldn't have had a problem taking it out myself, but this whole situation left me very curious.

Everything around me seemed so real. If nobody had ever mentioned that I was part of an experiment, I would have never questioned whether any of this was actually happening. I chose to close my eyes while she pulled out the needle because I wanted to know if everything I was experiencing was controlled by my vision.

I felt her rubbing my hand just after I woke up, so I knew I could interact and feel other people, but I had been looking at our hands at the time. If I were to have my eyes closed, would I be able to sense the moment when the needle was disconnected from my arm?

I heard the sound of her wheels crossing the floor, and then a few seconds later I did indeed feel the slight pull of the needle as it slipped out of my skin. I opened my eyes to see her once again right in front of me.

"Where are my manners?" she asked. "I'm so sorry. I never even told you who I am. My name is June."

"Miles Casey." I wanted to ask her all kinds of questions, beginning with whether she was real, but that seemed extremely rude.

I lifted the bed sheets a few inches to make sure I was wearing pants, and when I saw that I was wearing a new pair of sweatpants to go along with my plain blue t-shirt, I pulled the blankets off and rested my bare feet onto the cold linoleum floor. I tested my legs for just a second to make sure walking around in this world felt the way I expected it to, and when I felt confident nothing had changed, I stood and moved past June toward the open door. I gasped in awe as I stepped out onto the small balcony.

"Nothing beats an ocean sunset," June said as she muscled her chair over the doorframe tracks and onto the balcony alongside me. "Unfortunately, you won't see much of one today. The marine layer gets thicker as the evening goes, so by the time the sun sets tonight, you'll be lucky if you even see the orange glow through the clouds. Maybe tomorrow will be clearer."

"I think it's stunning just how it is," I said.

I pulled my eyes away from the horizon and looked up and down the beach. One man could be seen jogging away from us. A small family sat together on the wet sand as they dug into it with their small shovels, building a mound that would certainly become a sandcastle until the tide would reach it to wash it all away. An older lady walked slowly as two small dogs ran circles around her.

I felt an arm slip around my waist, and I turned to see June leaning into me. "I'm so excited for you to be here. I have been asking them for months now when we would be ready to begin the new phase and they just kept saying, 'Soon, June. Soon.' That's all they kept saying. But they would never tell me what 'soon' meant. I didn't know if it meant a few more days, or weeks, or years. I don't think they were trying to be rudely vague. I think they didn't know either and that's why they couldn't tell me. But I'm so glad you're here. I'm so glad we can start now with the new stuff."

"New stuff?" I asked. "I'm afraid I don't even know what's going on."

"I suppose that's expected. At least to some extent. They call this an experiment, and I guess it works better if you're at least a little bit in the dark." She must have noticed the flash of concern in my eyes because she continued, "Oh, honey. There's no need to be worried. Nobody's gonna hurt you or make you do anything you don't want to do. Z and Subi are really good people."

"They're the ones who are running this whole ... experiment? Z and Subi?"

"Yeah. They're great. I was told you already met them back in Idaho. Weren't they the ones who asked if you wanted to come here?"

"I met two people about my same age—in their mid-twenties. Summer and Ramsey, I think."

She nodded. "Yeah. That's them. Around here they don't go by Summer or Ramsey, though. Summer is Subi, and Ramsey is Z."

"I guess Z makes sense to be short for the name Ramsey, but how does Summer turn into Soo-Bee?"

"Her last name is Bishop. For a while, Summer went by Sue, but that didn't quite stick. It became Sue B. And that name stuck, but eventually everyone started spelling it S-U-B-I. She's amazing. You're gonna love her. They don't come any sweeter or smarter than Subi. Oooh, boy, the smarts of that young lady. A lot of geniuses are dumb when it comes to talking to other people." June rapped her knuckles onto the side of her head. "Dumb when it comes to relationships. And a lot of people who are the sweetest people in the world couldn't solve a two-piece puzzle. But that Subi—she's a genius and she's as kind-hearted as Mother Teresa."

"So, Ramsey and—I mean, Z and Subi pop in to see how things are going?" I asked, wondering how often they would directly pop into this Matrix world.

"Pop in? They live here. They both do. Z's house is the bigger one right behind this hotel. Subi's place is next to his. Smaller. Quaint. In fact, I was supposed to radio them when you woke up, but I wanted you all to myself for a few minutes." She chuckled like she had just revealed a sinister secret.

She pulled a small walkie-talkie out of a pouch on the side of her chair and notified someone on the other end that "the boy is awake."

They were on their way over here now. I was a lot less nervous now about whatever this experiment was than before, but I was not any less confused. Maybe now I would finally get a few answers.

FOUR

I took a seat in one of the two heavy plastic chairs on my balcony and continued to look over the railing at life happening along the shoreline. I marveled at the detail of it all, and I wondered if this scene was going to be different each day. Maybe the Matrix programmers would only have so many different scenarios to pull from and two weeks from now I may look over the balcony to see this exact scene again. Or maybe they had the ability to mix it up and I would see that grandma and her two dogs again on a different day, but the family building their sandcastle wouldn't be there. Then again, perhaps the artificial intelligence element of world building had infinite options, and each day would be different.

Seagulls began to swarm in front of us. Most of them remained in the air, circling around, back and forth at the height of our room, while others paced the sand below.

"They're my fault." June chuckled, pointing around at all the seagulls.

"How so?" I asked.

"I've been in charge of watching you sleep most of the time over the last five days. I like birds. All kinds of birds. A lot of people think seagulls are pests and dirty, but I could just sit here and watch them all day. The way they glide in the air. The way they know how to work with the air on a super windy day. Their funny personalities as they navigate their pecking order and fight over food."

She spun her chair around and wheeled back into the room, crossed over to the mini-fridge, and returned with the bag of bread that had been sitting on top of it. She broke the bread into small pieces and placed them about six inches apart along the balcony's railing. Once the pieces were lined up from one end to the other, she backed her chair up against the glass wall.

"I like to guess which bird is going to be brave enough first to perch on the balcony. My money is on that white one right there." She pointed a finger at one of the birds closest to us.

I decided to play along. "I'll take the dark gray one that's just hovering in the wind there," and I pointed a finger at my selected seagull.

She wore the biggest grin while we waited for something to happen. I was sure I would have plenty of time to get to know her over the coming months, but I had to wonder what her story was. Whatever it was in her history that put her in this chair didn't seem to affect her upper body, so I was guessing it was not a full-body degenerative disease. Maybe it was a spinal injury. Either way, someone this chipper must have come to accept her state a long time ago.

Then again, was June even real? If this experiment was meant to help convicts learn empathy and life skills, then it would make sense to give me someone in a wheelchair as a friend. Maybe I would spend my day interacting with all kinds of people who would require my help in one way or another.

The seagull I had picked out began to hover closer and closer to us until it dove right at the rail. It snatched quickly at the bread, knocking a few pieces down to the gulls below, and successfully flew away with one piece for himself.

I glanced at June expecting her to say I was right, but she just shook her head. "Nope. Doesn't count. Your bird didn't perch on the rail. It has to be brave enough to perch."

I couldn't help but smile. She clearly had this funny game fully organized with her own rules.

"Knock knock," a female voice said behind us.

We turned to see Subi and Z walking through the room. They stepped through the open door and joined us on the balcony.

"Look who's awake," Z said with a broad smile. "Are you feeling all right?"

I nodded and shrugged my shoulders. "Yeah. Maybe a little tired still, but my head is clearing up pretty well."

"Good!" Subi said. "We're all excited to have you join our team, but nobody is more excited than June. I'm sure she's told you all about the new phase."

"No, not really." I turned to look at June, who was wringing her hands with excitement.

June slapped her legs with both hands. "Hopefully I'll be walking by the end of the day. On my own legs. On my own two feet. Walking!"

"And ... My presence here is somehow going to make it so you can walk?" I was definitely confused.

"You'll be taking over her old job of mapping the area," Subi said. "You see, we need someone to do the painstaking task of collecting as much data as possible with the surrounding landscape. The more area we can feed into the system, the more detailed the world can be for those living inside of it."

"Not just more detailed," Z said, "but also cover a wider area."

"It seems pretty real to me," I said. "The detail is amazing."

They all laughed at once.

"No. No. No," Z said. "Everything you see right now is 100% real. You haven't plugged into Olinc yet."

"Olinc? What's that mean?" I asked.

"The alternate world we have built," Subi said. "We used to call it Our Lincoln City because it's our own little version of Lincoln City. That got shortened to Our Lincoln, and now everyone just calls it Olinc."

"Right now, there are only a few people who can plug into Olinc," Z said. "You are one of them." He tapped the spot just behind his ear. "Over time, more and more people will be able to plug into Olinc from anywhere in the world."

I felt that same spot at the base of my skull and found that there was a small circular piece about the size and shape of a coin just beneath the surface of my skin. There was also a line of stitches that, from the way it felt to my fingertips, I assumed they were about ready to be removed.

"So," I said, "whatever this thing is you implanted in the back of my neck—that's what makes it possible for me to plug into Olinc? And if someone in India or Australia had this same thing, they could plug in, and they would be able to be in the system?"

"That's right," Z said.

"Or in my case," June said, "Once I'm plugged in, my mind will be able to take me anywhere inside Olinc I want to go. I will be able to stand on my own two feet."

"June is going to be able to walk on her own two feet?" I marveled. "That's really cool!"

"In theory, yes," Subi said. "I have already gotten many of the bugs worked out. I think."

"Subi successfully plugged June into Olinc about a month ago," Z said. "The trick is going to be for Subi to figure out how to make it so June's Olinc body can function slightly different than her natural body."

"I think I'm there," Subi said. "I think I've successfully connected all the dots. The trick is that the whole system is meticulously designed to read and understand the minute details of the real world. That's the 'artificial intelligence' part of the system at work. It is constantly collecting data and constantly learning. My job has been to show it *how* to learn and *what* to learn. I want Olinc to be exactly like Lincoln City, or at least as close as possible. The system has also been learning every tiny detail it can about June herself. The hard part is to get the system to behave exactly the same with everything else, but to allow June to be slightly different."

"Very precise to reality," Z said. "So, there will be no dragons in Olinc. The west coast of Oregon isn't exactly tornado alley either, so no tornadoes here."

"And since it is mirroring reality," Subi said, "Every time it rains outside, it rains in Olinc in the same way. If you are inside Olinc and you get rained on during January, you will feel just as cold and wet as if it happened to you in the natural world."

"But if I know when I'm plugged in, then I'll know it's not real," I said. "I mean, if I'm inside Olinc, and I get rained on, then wouldn't it be kind of like realizing I'm in a dream while I'm in a dream? If I know it's not real, can't I just decide I'm not cold?"

Subi shook her head. "That's not how the brain works. If a dentist starts drilling into your tooth, you are going to feel a crazy amount of pain, but you are not actually feeling your tooth hurt."

"I'm not?" I asked.

"No," Subi said. "The nerves in your tooth are connected to other nerves, and more nerves, and more. And there's a chain of nerves all the way to your brain. You are not actually listening to what your tooth has to say. You are listening to what that last nerve in the chain has to say to your brain."

"Like a telephone," Z said. "You don't actually talk to your mom on the phone. You're talking to a piece of plastic and metal in your hand. If your mom were to say something on the other end, but Subi was able to change what those words were, and you were to hear only what Subi wants you to hear, and in your mom's voice—you wouldn't know any different. You would hear your mom say exactly what Subi wants you to hear."

June leaned forward in her chair and pointed a thumb at her lower back. "And in my case, there is a disconnect in my nerve chain. Everything below my waist doesn't connect to my brain. Not since the accident. Subi is going to reconnect that chain in Olinc."

"Sounds complicated," I said.

Z slapped me lightly on the shoulder. "You're asking all the same questions I used to ask before I gave up trying to understand. Now I just say to myself, 'Well, if Subi thinks it's possible, it's possible. How we get there will be between her and her smarts.'"

June spun in her chair and waved one hand in the air. "Chit-chat. Chit-chat. Chit-chat. Too much talking. Let's get down to my room. I've been wishing for this moment for twelve years now." And with that, she pushed over the tracks of the door frame and wheeled across the room.

I waited till the others had gone ahead of me, and I followed up the rear. We exited through the front door of my room, which opened up again to a balcony that spanned the width of the third floor. It wasn't until now that I got a glimpse of the building I had been in. Just like my room had suggested, the outside also looked like an older medium-priced hotel. There was a fourth floor above us, and with roughly twenty-five rooms on each floor, that made out to be somewhere in the ballpark of 100 rooms.

This was completely different than anything I had expected.

"Can I ask something?" I said after we made it into the elevator at the center of the building.

June pushed the button and was the first through the doors.

"You want to know why we chose you," Z said.

"Well, yeah," I said. "I mean, I'm not complaining. This all seems much better than whatever my fate was going to be after standing in front of a judge, but ..."

"Too good to be true, isn't it?" Z smiled. "Well, I fully admit. I didn't want to pick you. I wanted someone who was a bit more of a troublemaker. You look too ..." He thought for a moment.

"Boring," I said smiling, finishing his sentence for him.

Z returned the smile. "Subi and I both have the vision of using this platform to better people's lives. As it develops, all kinds of doors will be opened to make real change in the world. Real change. Think of it. If someone were to grow up in the projects of downtown Oakland or Chicago or even Johannesburg, and they never knew anything other than prostitutes and drug deals and gunshots, and we could plug them into Olinc, we could show them something completely different than what they have always known. We could fill some of these rooms with people on hospice, or people with whatever kinds of special needs, and let the convict take care of them in hopes of generating some real empathy and love for others. It would help rehabilitate the convict as much as help those who need assistance."

"There are a lot of different avenues where this could go," I said.

Z nodded. "And don't get me wrong. We plan to make an awful lot of money in the process. This was a fully functioning hotel called the Seaside Hotel when we bought it, and once things are rolling, we plan to fill it with people from all around the world who just want to take a quick vacation to the Oregon coast without having to spend hours on a plane. And that will help fund all of what we want to accomplish. But, for me, the real adventure is taking one person and remolding them into someone new. Money is nice, but people are much more interesting. Much more exciting. Much more fun."

The elevator sounded with a *ding* and the doors slid open. Subi reached to grab the handles on the back of June's chair as if she was going to push her out the door, but June wheeled out of there too quickly for anyone to offer any help.

She pulled up next to the room closest to the elevator and said, "Twelve years!" She twisted the knob and pushed the door open. "For twelve years I've been waiting for today!"

FIVE

June lay on her bed with the biggest smile I had ever seen.

There was a machine at the side of her bed that looked like a hospital monitor. The exact same machine was next to my own bed upstairs. I had assumed mine had something to do with my recovery from implant surgery, but apparently this machine was what would connect someone to Olinc.

Subi picked up the end of a black wire that had a small round end about the size and shape of a quarter. When Subi pressed the end to a spot just behind June's ear, the wire latched on without any effort, which made me think the two ends were magnetic. I reached up behind my own head and traced the implant with the tip of my finger.

Finally, June grabbed a large CPAP-style mask that covered both her nose and mouth and slid it on. She immediately began grasping for the lunchbox-sized machine at her bedside trying to find the power button, and once it was turned on, she inhaled a large breath. Relief shone in her eyes.

"June, you silly lady," Z said. "Turn your breather on before you slide that thing onto your face. Are you trying to suffocate yourself?"

"Why does she need a breather in the first place?" I asked. "Does she stop breathing once she's plugged into the system?"

"Most people do just fine," Subi said. "Very few will ever need a breather, but June has severe sleep apnea. She manages just fine with a normal CPAP when she's sleeping at night." Subi pointed to another mask and a small machine on the other side of the bed. "But taking her brain out of normal mode can cause it to run a little weaker on some of its unconscious tasks. Once she's plugged in, her heart rate will immediately drop by twenty beats per minute. Her breathing will be shallower, so she needs that monster-truck breather instead of the wimpy CPAP mask she uses at night."

"But putting that mask on without turning it on is obviously a problem," I said.

"Right. If she's wearing it without it powered on," Subi said, "then it's completely sealed off. It's like smothering her with a pillow."

"And with that, should we give it a go?" Z asked.

June gave the room a big thumbs-up.

"I think we should all be inside Olinc when she comes through," Subi said. "This is going to be really exciting." She turned to me and added, "Miles, are you comfortable hooking yourself up?"

I wasn't comfortable with that idea at all, but I was too macho to admit it. "Sure. No problem. I just connect the black wire to my neck, and then ...?"

"And then just push the button on the clicker," Z said.

June held up a little black box about the size of a deck of cards. At the center of it was a single red button.

"Simple as that?" I asked.

"Simple as that," Z said. "And then when you want to leave Olinc, just push the button again. The clicker is how you get in, and the clicker is how you get back out."

After we all separated, I went up to my room alone where I connected myself to the machine just as I had seen June do, except without her monster truck CPAP mask, and I lay on the bed with the clicker in hand. I took a deep breath and said out loud to no one in particular, "Buckle your seatbelts, boys. Here we go."

I pushed the button. At the moment I had done so, I had been closer to the edge of the bed with my eyes on the monitor, but after clicking it I found myself lying directly in the center of the bed looking up at the ceiling. Everything around me looked basically the same, except that the machine next to me was now gone. There was no black wire connected to the back of my neck.

I rolled off the bed and looked around the room. I slipped my clicker into the front pocket of my jeans and then walked to the balcony to look out over the beach. The sun was slightly lower in the sky now than it had been when I was up here before. Other than that, the only difference was that everyone was gone. There was no family down there playing in the sand. No joggers. No dogs. The waves still continued to roll in. Seagulls still filled the sky.

I closed my eyes and took in a deep breath. I was surprised at the reality of the salty air. It smelled exactly like it should and felt refreshing in my lungs.

I hurried down the stairs to June's room where Z and Subi were already standing next to her bed. June was nowhere in sight, though.

"How was it?" Z asked.

"Rather ... uneventful," I said. "I don't know if I thought it would feel like being sucked into a tube, or going down a slide, or what, but it was just kind of like—" I snapped my fingers. "I pushed the button and suddenly, I'm in."

"Right. Uneventful is a good word for it," Z said.

I pointed down at the bed. "June is still not here. How do we let her know we are all here ready for her?"

Subi pulled her cell phone from her pocket and held it up. "I made it so texts and phone calls work both ways." She tapped onto the screen with her thumbs for a few seconds and then slid the phone back into her pocket.

Within a matter of seconds, June appeared on her bed, lying in the center of it and looking up at the ceiling just like I had done.

I wouldn't have thought it possible, but her smile broadened even more as she sat up.

She braced herself against the bed with her left hand. With her right she grabbed her pant legs and pulled her legs off the edge of the bed.

"I'm a bit rusty," June said, looking down at her legs. "It's like, imagine you spent your whole life speaking Russian as a child, and then someone picked you up and moved you to the United States and nobody ever spoke Russian to you anymore. Decades later, if you bump into someone speaking Russian, you're going to be a bit rusty. You would know it's in your brain somewhere, but it takes a minute to find it. My brain is trying to remember how to speak the language of legs and feet."

We all stood quietly and watched as she stared down at her feet, concentrating on her legs. Every few seconds I looked at the faces of Z and Subi before returning my attention to June. For the first minute or so, I seemed to be the only one worried that this wasn't happening immediately, but after a while, the faces of the others began to also show their concern.

"There! There it is!" June shouted so loudly that I jumped.

I hadn't seen anything happen at first. Nothing at all. But then I saw it. The big toe on her right foot moved just the tiniest amount. And then the same thing happened with her left foot.

"Both feet. They're both there. I can feel the cold floor on my feet." June cupped both hands over her face for a moment, and when she removed them, tears were beginning to well up in her eyes. "My feet are so cold. It's amazing."

It was the first time I could remember anyone being so glad to have cold feet.

Over the course of about ten minutes, she went from wiggling toes to fanning her toes apart, to lifting one leg up and putting it down. Then the big moment came. She grabbed Z's hand with her left, and Subi's hand with her right, and they helped her stand. Once they felt comfortable enough to do so, Subi let go first, followed by Z.

"They're there! I can feel them!" Tears were streaming down her cheeks now as she held her arms out to the side as if she were on a balance beam, even though she still had not taken a step. "Take my hands again. I want to walk down to the beach. I want to feel the sand between my toes."

"You sure you're up for it?" Z asked.

"What's the worst that could happen?" June asked. "I don't even care if I fall and break a hip right now. Nothing can ruin this moment for me."

Z grabbed again for her hand, but Subi took a step back and pulled out her phone. She immediately began recording and gestured for me to take her place at June's side, which I did.

"Can you see that video once you're outside of Olinc?" I asked. "Will she be able to send that to her friends?"

"Yup. It's all just data," Subi said, staring at her screen.

June took one deep breath before slowly lifting her right foot and putting it back down only about two inches in front of where it had been. Her second step with her left foot was just as slow as her first, but the third step seemed to come a little easier, and the fourth even more so. By the time we reached the front door, she had already made great improvement, and she didn't appear to have to concentrate nearly as hard as before.

We had made our way to the stairs that led down to the beach. Z radiated his nervousness, but June didn't seem to have a care in the world. She was like a child on Christmas morning, and every step was a new gift.

Once we reached the bottom of the stairs, June sank one bare foot into the sand and let out a small cry of joy. My feet were also bare since nobody had yet given me a pair of shoes, but the feeling of freezing cold January sand piercing my feet like a thousand tiny needles did not bring me any joy at all. I ignored my discomfort as June pulled her hand away from mine and took a few steps holding only onto Z's hand. She then pulled that hand away from his as well and walked gingerly with each step, still holding both hands out to each side like a toddler learning to balance.

Z and I continued to walk at her sides, but she soon shooed us away, saying, "I'm good now. I'm good. Let me do this on my own."

I looked back at Subi to see her still recording June's every movement with a cell phone and periodically wiping a tear from her eyes.

Half an hour later, after the sun had set and the overhead hotel lights took over the job of illuminating the beach, Subi and I went back inside. Subi grabbed a pair of socks and rubber boots from June's room and then ran them out to June.

Subi then beckoned me to follow her up to my room where we sat on the balcony to watch June below.

"We will get you some proper footwear tomorrow." Subi sat in a chair and put her feet up on the balcony railing.

I slid two pairs of socks over my freezing feet. "It's all good. I'll be fine for now with my own tennis shoes ... wherever those went."

"They're in your closet." She studied me for a moment. "Now tell me for real how you ended up in jail. You stood out like a sore thumb in that holding room, you know?"

"It was that obvious, huh? I guess I'm not very good at hiding it."

She said nothing in reply but just waited for me to gather my thoughts. I didn't know quite where to begin. The whole scenario was really embarrassing to me.

"I'm a real wimp when I get cold, especially when I'm both cold and wet," I said. "My pickup truck had been dead for a couple of days. I had three different mechanics look it over, and nobody could tell me what was wrong with it. Anyway, I was walking home from work, and it was already a cold night."

"You didn't have any money for a cab?"

"You're going to think I'm weird, but I have this thing against cabs. It's not like I won't take one if I need one, but if I don't think I need one ... if I can just walk, I'll usually just walk," I said. "I'm stupid, I know, especially because it was just barely warm enough to rain instead of snow, and it started to come down. And I mean, it began to rain really, really hard. And I still had about twenty minutes' worth of walking still ahead of me before I would be home." I smiled as I watched June down below, who had convinced Z to slow-dance with her. "Then when I made it to an intersection, I looked over at the car that had just pulled up next to me at the red light, and I could see through the window that it was Jason. I didn't even think; I just reacted. I started slapping his window to unlock the door, and when he did, I just jumped in."

"Why is Jason your friend, anyway?" Subi asked. "I mean, maybe I'm reading him a little harshly, but that guy doesn't seem like a very good guy. And you ... I just don't get it."

"Jason's not my friend. Not really." I shook my head. "We grew up together. We lived on the same street for most of our childhood and we were even best friends for a few years around third to fifth grade. Then once puberty hit and we started to grow into who we would become—ya know, he kind of went one way and I went mine. We weren't enemies or anything, but we stopped being friends around middle school. He had his group. I had mine."

"So, not friends enough that you would ever go out of your way to hang out with him, but friendly enough to jump into his car."

I shrugged. "I guess that sums it up pretty well."

"Okay, keep going. Explain what you were doing when you broke into that house. Why would you go do that with him?"

"I didn't know that was what we were doing. I never got out of the car." I lifted my feet and put them up on the railing. "From what I've been able to piece together—from what Jason told me while we were locked up—he was working as a valet parking attendant for one of the nice restaurants back home in Idaho. He made a habit of checking the GPS system whenever he parked a car to see how far away from the restaurant that person lived because people always enter their home address into those things. If the house was close and if he felt he had time while the owner of the car was inside eating, he would sometimes speed over to their house and, well, help himself to whatever he wanted to grab."

"Not exactly a foolproof plan, was it?" Subi snickered.

I closed my eyes and shook my head. "I'm an idiot, I know. I was so consumed with feeling so cold and wet that it didn't even register in my mind that he wouldn't be driving a BMW that was worth ten times what I paid for my pickup truck. He said he had to make one quick stop before he could drop me off. We pulled into the driveway, and he pushed the button attached to the sun visor for the garage door to open. We pulled into the garage. I sat there in the car while he sprinted into the house and returned within two or three minutes. I didn't even know he had taken something until later."

"A gold watch," Subi said.

I nodded. "And a pair of diamond earrings. Both from a dresser drawer. Later on, after we had gotten arrested, he said the key to not getting caught was to never take something that would be noticed right away. That way they would have a hard time pinning down the date of when it happened. And then, never to make the rookie mistake of taking them to a pawn shop."

Subi sat in silence after I finished my story. In my embarrassment, I kept from making eye contact for quite a while, and when I did finally look over at her, she had a smirk on her face that spoke volumes.

She dropped her feet off the railing and raised her eyebrows. "You're on the west coast of Oregon now. It's always raining, and it's always cold. If your habit is to break into someone's house every time you get cold and wet, we might as well just take you back to lockup right now."

I shook my head and let out a chuckle. Her teasing did help ease the tension a bit, which was nice.

"Even after he jumped back into the car, I was still too dense to realize anything was up," I said. "It wasn't until I saw that door at the back of the garage swing back open and there was this old grandma lady standing there with a double-barreled shotgun pointing straight at us. She slapped the button to close the garage door, and she swore like a sailor at us all the way up until the cops arrived at the house."

Subi was belly-laughing now.

"It's not that funny," I said, trying not to laugh along with her. "I've never been so scared in my life. That lady's hands were shaking all over the place. I was 100% convinced she was going to slip and pull the trigger."

Subi doubled over in her chair, struggling to catch her breath between fits of laughter.

"I'm so glad we got you for this experiment instead of Jason," she said once she was calm enough to speak. "I mean, Z speaks all nobly about wanting to help reform convicts and stuff, but I think that kind of goal needs to be tackled some other day in the future. Right now, we are still working out too many of the bugs. Right now, we need someone who is good for June. You're going to be her right-hand man. She always says she's willing to take on whatever challenges we want to throw at her, and she really is up for just about anything, but I didn't want her to have to worry about babysitting some troublemaker. At least not yet. Not right now. Let's have some fun with all these new experiences while things are developing."

"Have you said these things to Z?"

"Of course. We've gone rounds about these things many times. The problem is that his idea of fun and my idea of fun are not the same thing. He is a unique character."

She pointed a finger down at Z and June. June was attempting to skip now, and Z was standing directly in front of her, jogging backward with his hands out ready to catch her. When she did fall, she went face-down in the sand without him being able to stop her, but she just laughed and began again.

"He cares deeply for June," I said. "That's easy to see."

"That man cares very deeply for only a handful of people. Very, very deeply," she said before pausing, and adding almost under her breath, "Sometimes I wonder how far he would go to stand up for those he cares most about. I'm a little scared to find out just how far he would go in their defense."

"Are you telling me I need to be careful?" I asked, a bit alarmed.

She seemed to snap out of a bit of a reverie at me saying this. "Oh, no. No. No. I shouldn't have said that. You're not going to do anything to set him off like that, especially not to June. I shouldn't have said that."

I couldn't help but take a mental note, though, not to do anything to June that might upset Z. I couldn't see how that would be a problem anyway since June was such a sweetheart of a lady.

I still wasn't sure I understood what my role in this experiment was, but the majority of my fears were gone now that I was getting to know everyone. Tomorrow, I assumed, would answer most of my remaining questions.

SIX

After I clicked myself back into the real world, and after everyone else went back to their respective rooms, I sat alone on my balcony wrapped in extra layers of clothing and blankets. The ocean was soothing to my soul. It had always been that way for me, but I didn't grow up near any of the coasts, so being on the beach wasn't something I could do very often.

Watching and listening to the waves roll in was more enjoyable and a better way to wind down than any television program I could have chosen to end such an eventful day.

The next morning, even before grabbing a bite or taking a shower, I wrapped myself up again and was back on my balcony to watch the waves. The tide had come all the way up to the base of the building during the night, leaving the sand smooth like a blank canvas waiting for today's artists to cover it with footprints and sandcastles.

A few minutes before 8:00, I went down to the hotel's main lobby to meet with the team and learn what my main job would be. I entered through the front doors and found June, Subi, and Z already there waiting for me.

In front of the open chair that was obviously meant for me was a breakfast plate and a glass of orange juice. On the plate was an omelet covered in avocado along with two slices of wheat toast.

On the table next to my utensils was a credit card.

"Is this for me?" I asked as I picked up the card and then saw that it had my name on it. "What do I get to do with this?"

"Anything you want or need," Z said. "You're not here on salary or anything. You obviously get room and board here at the hotel, and whatever else you feel you need—"

"Ooh, imagine the parties I'll be able to throw with this," I said with a smile.

"Riiiiight," Z said sarcastically. When I looked at him in surprise, he laughed and added, "Why are you looking at me like that? You're boring. I've told you that before. You're never going to take that card to the bar to buy everyone a round. You're not going on some crazy shopping spree. We all know it."

He was right, of course. I had never been one for frivolity. I had always been more comfortable in a pair of Levi's and a T-shirt than I would be dressed to the nines like Z often was. And since the first idea that had popped into my head when I picked up the credit card was to find myself a good pair of boots that would keep my feet both warm and dry out on the beach, I knew Z was obviously right. I was boring.

The rundown of my duties was simple: My job was to experience the area.

Subi took a moment to explain how the implant in my head worked—most of which went right over my head. I did understand the basics of what she was saying, though, and that was that the implant inside of me was constantly reading my brain. The nervous system of my body fed my brain information at all times, and my implant had the ability to read that info as it came and went. So, everywhere I went, the data from everything I saw, touched, tasted, smelled, or heard would be read by the Olinc system. It didn't matter if I was close to the hotel or not.

Only June and I were equipped with this version of a chip, which they called the "mapping chip." Up to this point, the world of Olinc was restricted to the places June had been able to go. Being that she was in a wheelchair, she had not spent nearly as much time on the beaches as I would. She had spent countless hours experiencing the roads and neighborhoods of Lincoln City. She had also spent a lot of time inside all the stores and businesses to make Lincoln City as realistic as possible.

If one of us were to see a grocery store from the outside, then only the outside of the store would be seen while we were inside Olinc. Since she had spent so much time meticulously going up and down the aisles of those stores, though, if we were to visit the grocery store inside Olinc, we could snag ourselves a bag of cookies or a sandwich from the deli and be able to walk right on out of there without needing to pay. A sandwich from the deli in Olinc would go stale and moldy just like it would in the real world, but the system would automatically restock shelves to put another batch of sandwiches there for the next day.

"The Olinc system used to be strictly tied to the real world," Subi said. "If you were to go to the grocery store inside Olinc and take a gallon of milk, then there would be an empty spot on that milk shelf until June went back to that store with her mapping chip. As soon as she looked at the milk section in the real world, then everything inside Olinc would update and the milk shelves would be fully stocked again."

"But there was an obvious problem with that," June added. "With all the food items strictly programmed to be like the real world, then all the produce, and the dairy, and everything perishable in the grocery store was constantly going bad unless I spent half of my waking hours just in the grocery store. That wasn't much fun for me to always have to spend so much time at the grocery stores."

"It wasn't very practical either," Subi said.

"Not to mention the managers of the grocery stores in the area were all creeped out by this lady who was coming back and looking at all their fruits and vegetables every two or three days without buying anything," June said.

"It took me a while to figure it out, but I was able to change the programming on certain things," Subi said. "Now, every time someone with the mapping chip, just like you have, observes something, then your observation becomes the default state of that item. It is on a timer for one week. If nobody with the mapping chip views that item in the real world again within that week, then it will automatically update itself and revert to its default state. It will become just like it was a week ago. That way the bananas don't all go mushy. The milk doesn't go sour. The bread doesn't go moldy."

They went on to explain to me how I should observe the outside world. It would be important for me to experience the same thing in a variety of ways. The experience of visiting one of the nearby lighthouses in January would be different from visiting in July. Doing something in the morning would be different than the early afternoon, or evening, or in the dark. The artificial intelligence built into the system would do its best to guess the difference between visiting a location under different circumstances, but no amount of AI guessing was ever as good as the high quality, raw data I could feed it myself.

"Again, the settings inside Olinc are all tied to the real world," Subi said. "The system knows exactly how far to expect the tides to come in, and at what time. The weather patterns will adjust in real time according to what is going on outside."

"But the system does fill in a lot of the gaps," June said. "You won't have to go to the same place when the wind is ten miles per hour, and also eleven, and also twelve, etc. Nothing like that. If you're somewhere while it's calm, and in the same place while it's gusting stiffly, the system can guess the nuances of the changes in between those two. It's quite amazing."

I took a cab to go out shopping for some boots and wet weather clothing. While I was out running these errands, I found myself remembering the conversations I'd had back at the county jail. Clearly, one of the main reasons someone would be uncomfortable with this whole situation would be the fact that my own brain would be transmitting data all day long.

I had always found it creepy how, if I ever had a conversation about needing to buy a new bed, then I would automatically see advertisements for new beds everywhere I went. I hated how my cell phone and other devices were always monitoring everything I did and feeding that data to advertising companies.

This felt like the same thing, only a thousand times more intrusive.

That was more than a little unsettling to think about, but it was all for a good cause. Thinking about June taking those first steps brought such a smile to my face that it was easy for me to push past that discomfort and feel pride in the idea that I was helping to build this alternate place where the Junes of the world could dance along the shoreline.

That same shoreline was where I first began spending what I would call my "experience time." I thought it would be best to spend time close to the hotel where June and her wheelchair weren't able to do much.

That would work out great for me. I could easily see myself taking a walk along the waterline every day, in either direction, and getting to experience every nook and cranny of the beach.

I was especially excited about low tide. I had seen a low tide from my balcony and was interested in exploring the rock formations that were exposed when the waterline was so low.

It was while I was standing atop one of the large rocks that I happened to look up at the Seaside Hotel about a mile away. There was a man on the balcony of one of the rooms of the fourth floor. He was sitting atop the balcony's railing, facing the water with both feet hanging down. It brought chills to my body to think of how one wrong move would send him crashing down about sixty-five feet to the concrete ledge below.

He fascinated me for so many reasons. Who was he? I thought only June and I were living in the hotel, but I guessed there were other people who had access to it. That made sense. The building was clean and well cared for. Clearly June wasn't doing it all. Subi and Z seemed too busy to focus on the upkeep of the building. Maybe that was this man's job. Maybe he was a maintenance man or janitor.

From so far away, it took me a minute to understand why he kept bringing one hand up to his face. Then I realized he must have a cigarette in his hand. That was pretty much the only thing he was doing. Every few minutes I couldn't help but glance back up at him as he remained motionless like a statue for nearly an hour, except for that one hand with the cigarette.

"Hello there," a voice called from behind me. "Just out exploring?"

I turned to see a police officer approaching me.

I was standing atop a large boulder that protruded from the sand where I had been observing the large starfish and sea anemones around the rock formation. I retracted a little at the sight of the officer. There were people up and down this beach. Why had he come this far out of his way just to talk to me?

"I'm sorry. Am I not supposed to be climbing on these rocks?" I asked. "I swear, I haven't hurt any of the starfish or sea life."

He smiled. "You're not in any kind of trouble. There's nothing wrong with climbing on the rocks. I just wanted to come see how you're doing and introduce myself. My name is Officer McKnight."

This was all very confusing. "I'm fine, I guess."

"You're staying at the Seaside Hotel, am I right? You're the new guy there?"

"Yes." I looked back at the hotel and noticed that the man on the top floor was no longer sitting on his balcony.

"Are they treating you okay over there?"

"Are they treating me okay? Yes. They're all very nice," I said. "Can I ask why you're asking me these things?"

A female voice sounded through his radio system, and he paused for a moment to listen before returning his attention to me. "This is a rather small town. Not a lot goes on in this town that I don't know about. I'm aware of the project that is going on at the Seaside Hotel. It has the ability to change the dynamics of the city, especially if they are taking people out of jail from other states and bringing them over here."

We stared at each other for a moment without either of us saying anything. He was reading me, and I was reading him.

"You don't look like you're much trouble, though," he said. "You seem all right to me."

"I appreciate that. You won't get any trouble from me."

"That's what I like to hear," he said, but then his mood changed. "Look, there are a lot of question marks floating over this whole operation. There are a lot of things we don't quite understand." He looked to his left and right as if he were making sure nobody else could hear. "Most importantly, there are things *you* don't understand about what is going on around here. I know they're keeping a lot of secrets from you."

"Like what?" I genuinely wondered.

He shook his head. "I wish I could tell you. Some things I know, but I'm not at liberty to say. Other things, I simply don't know. One thing I do know, though, is that you look like you're a good guy. Stay that way. Keep your nose clean. Keep your head above water. Don't let yourself get tangled up in anything."

I had nothing to say to that, so I just stood there in silence until he reached into his breast pocket and pulled out a card. He held it out to me. I jumped down from my rock and began walking through the four inches of water back toward him.

Unexpectedly, a larger wave pushed at me from behind and came almost all the way up to my knee. Freezing water came pouring into the tops of both my boots, filling them past my ankles. I let out a loud grunt at the feeling of my feet being suddenly engulfed in ice water.

"Ooh. I'm so sorry about that," Officer McKnight said with a grimace. "We have all been there many times. That's no fun."

I took the card from his hand and jammed it into my pocket without even looking at it. I wanted nothing more now than for him to go away, and for me to be back in my own room for a hot shower.

I hurried a few steps away from the waterline and sat down on the wet sand. I pulled off my boots and dumped out the water. I then took off my wet socks and wrung them out, which did nothing to make them more comfortable. When I had looked back at the hotel before, it didn't seem so far away, but now that my feet were screaming at me in frigid pain, the idea of walking back felt like a ten-mile trek through the Arctic.

I heard the officer say something about giving him a call if I ever needed anything as I hurried away.

Each step was worse than the one before it. By the time I reached the steps that led up to my room, every inch of me felt miserable, especially my feet.

In my room, I filled the tub with six inches of lukewarm water and sat on the edge with only my feet submerged. Once I could feel my toes again, I turned on the shower and was glad a hotel this size would surely have a water heater large enough that I could stay in here as long as I wanted without having to worry about it running out.

Once my fingertips had begun to raisin, I decided it was time to step out.

I noticed the little green light blinking on my cell phone indicating there was an unread text message. I opened it to find that it was from June informing me there was pizza in the main lobby if I wanted to join them.

Although my body temperature felt like it was back up, I still put on an extra pair of socks as well as my dry tennis shoes.

As I descended the stairs to the main lobby, I resolved to go out shopping again the next day for a second pair of boots so I could let one pair dry out completely before I would have to put them back on. I also thought it would be nice to have a pair of soft, warm slippers I could wear on evenings such as this.

"How was your first day?" Subi asked as I stepped through the lobby doors.

"Cold," I shot back.

"Yeah, you looked pretty miserable coming in," Z said. "I saw what happened when that wave came into your boots. We have all been there many times. Waterproof boots are the best at keeping water out, but when water does get inside, it's the absolute worst!"

I approached the table and saw a large pizza box. I flipped the lid open and grabbed a slice of Meat Lover's.

"Tie-Dye Pizza is the best pizza place in Lincoln City," Z said.

"It's so good," I said through a mouthful of pizza.

"Have a seat." Z pointed at the open chair directly across from him at the table. "So ... I saw that a police officer approached you on the beach today."

I looked up at him, and then around at Subi and June. All three of them seemed quite interested in where this conversation was about to go.

"What was that about? Did he say anything?" Z asked.

"Did he say anything about what?" I asked.

"Why was he interested in you?" Z said.

"He said he likes to keep tabs on everything that goes on in town. He said he knew there was a new guy at this hotel, and he wanted to meet the new guy," I said. "That was pretty much it."

Z looked around at the other two before looking back at me. "Did he say why he was interested in meeting the new guy?"

I shook my head. "Not really. I kind of freaked out with the water in my boots before we had much of a conversation. He said something about how he knew that whatever we were doing had the ability to change the town, especially if we were bringing in criminals from other states, but for the most part I think he was just checking in on me to make sure I was okay."

Z quickly changed the subject to something lighthearted. We spent the next hour or so just laughing together and enjoying each other's company over a few more slices of pizza, although Z and Subi had already eaten, so June and I were the only ones working on the pie in front of us.

As I sat on my balcony that night, I couldn't help but repeatedly run over the two very short conversations that had taken place that day. Officer McKnight really hadn't said all that much to me, but the fact that he had taken an interest in me in the first place made me wonder what he knew that I didn't. I came into this experiment fully aware that there would be aspects of my life that kept me in the dark, but it added another layer of discomfort to know the local police were keeping tabs on whatever those dark places were. And when Z came to me wanting reassurance that nobody had removed my blindfold, the whole situation became a little more unnerving.

SEVEN

I pulled back from the rest of the group for the remainder of the week. I went down to the main kitchen early in the morning to make myself something to eat and was out of there with a sack lunch in hand before anyone else was awake to join me. I ate my lunch at whatever location I was exploring for the day and then kept my eye on the main lobby to wait for it to clear before going down for whatever leftovers I could scrounge up.

It wasn't that I didn't like the other people. That wasn't the case at all. I was just beginning to feel the weight of the uncertainty surrounding my life. I felt like I had been tossed off the boat right into the deep waters and was being told to swim. Taking this step back gave me a few days to reset, and when I felt ready, I would start wading back into the social aspects of the group again.

That came to an end on Sunday night as I was sitting on my balcony with a cup of hot tea in my hands.

I heard a knock at my door. I opened it up to see Subi and Z both standing there with their typical friendly smiles. Z was empty handed, but Subi was holding a thick blanket under her arm.

I welcomed them in, and they joined me out on the balcony. Subi took the second chair. I offered to bring out one of the chairs from inside my room, but Z chose to stand.

We chatted about little things for a while before we found ourselves back on the topic of what had gotten me in trouble with law enforcement back in Idaho. I realized this was the first time Z had heard it from me. I was slightly less embarrassed than when I had told Subi since I already knew she believed me and found it hilarious.

As I was getting into the thick of the details, however, I could tell Z wasn't buying it. He didn't interrupt me or roll his eyes, but he also wasn't trying very hard to hide his skepticism.

"You don't believe him, do you?" Subi accused.

"I didn't say that," Z said. "I didn't say anything."

"Okay, well, then say it. Do you believe him?" Subi asked.

"Innocent until proven guilty," Z said as he turned and looked out over the water.

"That's dumb," Subi said. "Come on. Don't give us that. He has done everything you've asked of him. He's up early in the morning and gets right to work, and he keeps at it the entire day. He has never used the credit card on anything but the essentials. What could there possibly be about Miles that you deem untrustworthy?"

"Okay, if you wanna go there, let's go there," Z said. "Nobody is that dumb. He wants us to believe he just happened to jump in the car with some guy who wasn't his friend, and he happened to end up in the garage of a stranger while his friend was inside grabbing things. Every jail and prison is full of people who say they were innocent and just happened to be in the wrong place at the wrong time."

Subi threw up her hands. "You're impossible. How do you even function in this world without any level of trust?"

"We snatched Miles right out of the hands of the jail guards," Z shot back, "and you immediately believe every word that comes out of his mouth. I don't know how *you* function in this world."

I sat silently between the two of them, Z on my left as he leaned forward against the railing and Subi to my right sitting in the other chair. It was a strange feeling to have two people fighting over me as if I weren't even present.

After a few minutes of complete silence, other than the sounds of the waves crashing down below, Z took a step toward the open sliding glass door. "It's too cold to just hang out here." He stepped through into the room. "Miles, you seem like a good guy. I hope you prove me wrong about not believing your story. Time will tell."

I expected Subi to also take her exit as soon as Z left, but when she showed no signs of wanting to call it a night, I slid the door closed behind him.

"So, Miles, what makes you tick?" she asked.

"What?"

"What makes you tick? What keeps you going? What are your favorite things in life?"

"Well, I'm a typical guy, I suppose. I like watching sports. Listening to music. Being outside."

"Those are generic answers," she accused with a bit of a laugh. "Let's hear some specifics."

"Okay. I like the Seattle Mariners, even though their goal every year seems to be to come as close as possible to making the playoffs without actually getting there. I hate the Yankees with almost as much passion."

"Now we're talking." Subi smiled. "Keep it coming."

"A lot of my friends poke fun at me because I don't listen to any of the new music that's out these days. I like the old stuff."

"Me too! I think the best music began around the time of The Beatles. In those early days there were only a few good bands. By the time the '70s rolled around, things were really flowing. Really creative. Really amazing."

"And then when AI began to get involved with music, it all went to blah!"

"Blah! Exactly," she said. "I refuse to listen to AI music, except ..."

"Except what?" I asked once I realized she wasn't going to finish that sentence.

"Except ... I refuse to listen to any of the music that has been generated through AI to sound like it was written by the Beatles. I hate that. I know that garbage was made long after the Beatles had died, so it takes all the art out of music for me." Her lips curled up into a sheepish grin. "But I have to admit there are times when I will listen to the Beatles sing some of my other favorite songs—ones they never wrote."

"So, you won't listen to any songs that someone created with AI to make it sound like the Beatles wrote it, but you will listen to an AI version of the Beatles singing a Michael Jackson song?" I laughed.

"I know. I know." She laughed along with me. "That makes me sound like I play both sides of the fence with AI music, but there are just some really fun combinations. My favorite one lately is to have the Beach Boys sing Metallica's 'Enter Sandman.'"

I laughed. "I admit, I've never tried that combination."

"So, what's your favorite album of all time?" she asked.

"I really like the progressive music from the '70s, '80s, and '90s."

"Progressive music? What's that? Like, the bands sang about politically progressive things or something?"

"No. Not politically progressive. Progressive music is the kind of music that is put together with lots of changes and movements in the music. You know how songs like 'Stairway to Heaven' and 'Carry On Wayward Son' were really long songs that would change tempos and moods throughout the whole song?"

"Yeah. That's good stuff."

"Those are the types of songs that are considered progressive. The music progresses throughout. So, consequently, because the songs tend to be eight minutes or more, those types of songs were not on the radio very much. And since they weren't on the radio very much, most people didn't know they even existed."

"Most of your favorite bands were bands I wouldn't know, then," she said.

"Well, I still loved a lot of the radio bands, but it was bands like Dream Theater and Vanden Plas that I really love the most."

"You're right. I've never heard of them. I'll have to give them a listen." She pulled out her phone. "Text me the names of those two bands."

Subi stayed with me out on the balcony late into the night. I knew she was as cold as I was because she continually pulled her blanket tighter around her body. Throughout the entire conversation, I wondered how long she would want to stay. During the quiet moments, while we were between topics, I found myself scrambling for something new to bring up in hopes that she would stay a little longer.

After she was gone, I lay in bed looking up at the ceiling. It was nice to have a friend. It was nice to have someone I enjoyed spending time with, even if that someone wore a wedding ring at times. She hadn't worn it at all since I had arrived in Oregon, which I thought was quite strange, but I clearly remembered it on her finger back in Idaho.

Perhaps that was one of the nicer things about having her as a friend. I knew she was off the market, so there was no temptation to think about where things could possibly go between us.

When morning came, I began my day again by stepping out onto my balcony to take in some fresh sea air. Along with the sound of seagulls squawking in the distance, I heard a sound from up above me. I leaned over the railing and looked up to see that man up on the top corner balcony. He was again sitting dangerously on the edge of his railing. When I had seen him from a distance, his posture looked a bit scary. Seeing it this close was downright terrifying.

"Are you okay up there?" I yelled.

"Who's there?" he answered back but never turned his head to look at me.

"My name is Miles."

"You're the new boy." His eyes remained forward as he looked out over the ocean.

"Yeah. I'm the new guy. What's your name? Do you live here?"

He leaned back and swung his legs back over the railing. He disappeared from my view, but I still heard his voice call out, "Come up here a minute. I want to talk to you."

I climbed the stairs and found my way to the last room at the end of the building. The door was already cracked open, so I opened it the rest of the way as I knocked.

"Miles, you say?" the man asked as he stood in the center of the room.

His voice did not match his stature. He was of average height, but his voice resonated gruffly and deeply from so many decades of cigarettes.

He was a thin man with a short unkempt gray beard and hair pulled back into a simple ponytail. He wore a pair of dark sunglasses. He looked to be in his sixties. Other than the heavy smell of cigarette smoke in the air, the room was kept relatively clean.

Even with his dark sunglasses, I could tell his eyes were not fixed on me. It was as if he were looking beyond me. It was in that moment that I realized he must be blind.

"Yes, sir. I'm Miles."

He waved away my words and felt his way to a seat in the corner next to a small table just like the one in my own room. "No need to call me 'sir.' Amos is the name. Just Amos."

"It's nice to meet you, Amos."

Amos placed his cigarette into his mouth and then reached into his pocket. He pulled out a fresh pack of cigarettes and peeled off the plastic wrapper. He then retrieved a single cigarette from the pack and then pressed its tip to the one already in his mouth until the ends of both were glowing. He took one last drag from the shorter cigarette before tamping it out in an ashtray.

"What do you think of this place?" he asked.

"It's nice. No complaints so far."

"Did they tell you that you are part of an experiment? Did they tell you that's why they brought you here?"

"They told me that, yeah," I said. Even though I had spent a good portion of the week wrestling with the idea of being a source of data collection, I didn't want to let that show. Something about him made me immediately feel like I needed to choose a side between him and the others, so I added, "I agreed to the terms. I'm going to see this through."

"You did not agree to any terms. How could you agree to any terms if you don't even know what's going on?" He placed the cigarette on the edge of the ashtray without extinguishing it. "Let me guess. I bet they told you that chip in the back of your skull is there just to read your senses. What you smell. What you see. Taste. Feel. Hear."

"That's right. You think they're lying to me?"

"Yeah. They *are* lying to us. To all three of us. To you. Me. That one in the wheelchair."

"All three of us? You're in this too?"

"I guess you could call me the failed part of the experiment. That is why they did not even bother to mention to you that I exist, or that I am part of this too." He smiled for the first time, exposing spotted yellow teeth for only a second before his face went somber again. "I don't buy what they are selling us. I may be blind in the eyes, but I'm obviously the only one who sees right through them."

"Like what? What do you know that they're keeping from me?"

"They put an implant in your brain to read what your brain is doing. They even tell you they're experimenting on you. Do you honestly believe they are only interested in what you smell and see?" He shook his head vigorously. "Nah. They want to know what you *think.* They want to know what you *feel.* They want to read you like a book. Everything about you. Everything."

"Let's suppose that's true. What would they even do with that kind of information?"

He shrugged. "I don't know. The only thing I do know is that I don't trust them. Whatever it is, it isn't good. Whatever it is, they don't want to tell you, or they would have told you already. But they keep you in the dark. How dumb do you have to be to think they are on your side when they keep you in the dark? Huh?"

He had a point. I couldn't think of any time when someone was working in my best interest while refusing to fully tell me what they were up to.

I noticed the machine next to his bed that could connect him to Olinc.

"When you hook yourself up to Olinc, can you see? Are you still blind?" I asked.

"When I hook myself up to Olinc?" He scoffed. "I have never hooked myself up to Olinc. I don't trust it."

"I saw June walk again. It was her first time walking in ... I think it was twelve years."

"She isn't really walking. Not really."

"It feels real to her. That's something."

"That's nothing." He retrieved his cigarette from the ashtray and placed it in his lips.

"So ... you're not even curious enough to try. You're not even interested enough to see what it's like in Olinc? I've been inside. It's very natural and realistic."

"Nope," he said matter-of-factly. "I'm not giving them the satisfaction. I admit it would surely be nice to see again. But everything comes at a cost. If I give them that, they will ask for something equally big in return. Maybe bigger. I don't want to find out what kind of debt they expect me to repay if I hook up to their machine. I don't trust any of them. I don't even trust the lady in the wheelchair."

"They've never asked much from me so far. Just some help collecting data to build Olinc."

"You're simple, aren't you?" He laughed. "That's always how these things start. Everything is always free at first. They give you something and ask for nothing in return. Then one day they show up with a list of what they have given you and they tell you it is time to pay up."

My mind was deeply unsettled when I left Amos's room. So much so that I just stood there right outside his door for at least a few minutes as I processed my thoughts.

When I looked back up again, I saw something out in the parking lot that took me by complete surprise. It was Z. He was leaning up against a pickup truck. Not just any pickup truck, though. It was a thirty-year-old Ford F-150. Tan in color with double maroon stripes down the length of it, and more dents than would be possible to count. It was *my* pickup truck.

Z looked hilarious in his double-breasted pin-striped suit, leaning up against my old ride. Those two didn't match.

"How on earth—" I cried out as I sprinted down the steps, skipping many of them as I went.

"I thought you'd like a little piece of home," Z said with a smile. "And when I saw that look in your eye every time you called for a cab to run your errands, I knew this was gonna be a nice surprise."

I jumped into the cab and found the keys already in the ignition. I turned the key and the engine roared to life. "How is this possible? How is it running? I had three different mechanics try to figure out what was wrong with it. Nobody could—"

"I know a lot of people in Idaho. A lot of really talented people owe me a lot of favors."

And with that, I realized I could add one more big item to the growing list of favors that had been done for me.

EIGHT

I loved having my truck back. For the first week, it seemed like every time I drove it, I would notice something new that had been done to it. There were obvious things, of course, like the fact that it wasn't running at all when I left it back in Idaho, but there were more subtle things as well. The gears shifted smoothly now, and when I asked Z about it, he just grinned and said, "You needed a whole new transmission." That nasty brown stain that used to be on the passenger seat was gone, which I never thought could be possible. The truck even had all four hubcaps again.

My friends back home often poked fun at me because of my old Ford. I didn't mind. It was uniquely mine. I disliked traveling by cab so much that, while my truck was out of commission, it was common for me to walk for miles rather than to call for one.

When I was behind the wheel, I was in control of where I was going at all times. In my pickup truck, I had the ability to pop on my favorite tunes. Sure, I could still listen to the same music if I were riding in a cab, but in my own truck I didn't have to worry about my music being constantly interrupted by a twenty-second commercial about a fast-food restaurant or personal injury lawyer or something.

Over the course of the first few months, June and I came up with a dozen locations we thought would be great places to add to Olinc. These locations were all the types of places tourists would find interesting. June thought of them a bit differently than I did, though. She called them "Zen spots" because she could slip into Olinc, go to one of these places, and sit for long periods of time to meditate.

Of these Zen spots, her favorite was clearly the area around the Yaquina Head Lighthouse. Subi was in the room one morning as June was thanking me for spending so much of my observation time there.

"Let's go after dinner this evening," Subi said. "I haven't been over there in a long time."

"In person, or inside Olinc?" I asked.

Subi placed a hand on June's shoulder. "In Olinc, so all three of us can go."

I liked that idea. Inside Olinc, June had been taking a cab there for the last few days, but I had spent so much time in the area over the last month that I hadn't wanted to go for more than a week. I hadn't been there a single time inside Olinc to see how it was turning out. It was going to be nice to witness someone else enjoying my effort.

Inside Olinc, we all rode together in my pickup truck, which meant that there wasn't a whole lot of elbow room between us. I didn't mind.

"You know," Subi said, "Z and I were so caught up in trying to decide what kind of person to pick from the jail that we didn't think about the benefits of having a driver. The detail along this roadway is fantastic."

"I took a cab everywhere I went," June added. "Since the car takes me to my destination whether I'm watching the road or not, I have a tendency to daydream."

"I guess I hadn't thought much about that," I said. "Most people prefer to take a cab so they can just jump in, turn on their favorite podcast or movie, and let the GPS take them wherever they want to go. But me, I really prefer the feeling of being at the wheel."

"It shows." June looked high up into the trees as she spoke. "Even for those who are drivers, I think most people zone out and wouldn't take in the detail like you do. You're doing great work."

"It's going to be fun to see the world of Olinc grow larger and larger," I said.

Subi nodded. "Right now Olinc is just our area around the Oregon coast, and then a pretty good amount back home in Idaho."

"I didn't realize there were two locations," I said. "Are they connected?"

"Not very well. Soon enough. Z and I would like for—" Subi cut herself off.

"What? What is it?" I asked. "I'm happy to make the drive. I don't even mind making the long trip alone. I could do it once a week until you feel we have enough detail of the route."

"That's okay. There's no need to connect the two yet." She turned toward me in her seat. "Teach me to drive a stick!"

"You can't drive a stick?" I was a bit surprised. This brilliant girl was the kind who had already accomplished so much. How could it be she didn't know how to work a stick shift?

"I hardly even know how to drive an automatic. Half of my friends from high school still don't know how to drive. At least I have my license, even though I almost always order a cab," she said. "I'm always so busy that being in a cab is a nice way to get a few things done on my laptop. It's nice to be completely alone with no other people or distractions. If I were to spend an hour driving around town in my own car, then that would be an hour I didn't get anything accomplished. That would be an hour longer I would have to work once I got home."

"Okay, then. Just tell me when you want to start. I'll teach you."

"Why not today? Let's drop June off at the lighthouse and you'll teach me." Subi smiled. "And since we're doing it here in Olinc, if I drive the truck off a cliff and we end up at the bottom of the ocean, we'll just wake up in our beds."

"If we die inside Olinc, it just kicks us out?"

"In theory, yes."

"Just in theory?"

"Well, nobody has actually done it yet."

A nice thing about driving around in Olinc was that there were no other cars on the roads. Although the system included everything from stoplights to traffic signs, I could drive right through red lights, and I didn't have to worry about a car smashing into me from another direction. Inside the state park area around the lighthouse, it was sometimes hard to find a parking spot, but that was never the case inside Olinc.

We pulled up as close to the lighthouse as we could and let June step out. Within a few steps of being out of the truck, June began skipping and continued doing so until she chose a spot on the grass. She sat cross-legged, placed her hands on her knees, and closed her eyes.

"She really is a joy," I said. "Show me someone who doesn't like June, and I'll show you someone who has serious issues."

"Serious issues."

"Where did you guys find her?" I turned the truck around and headed back toward the main road. "I mean, she obviously didn't come from the county jail like I did, right?"

"She was our neighbor. Z and I have known her for many years."

"So, you knew her before her accident. I didn't realize you and Z were neighbors."

Subi nodded. "June used to babysit me when I was little. Since long before her accident. Z didn't move into the neighborhood until he was about ten or so."

"You and Z have been friends for quite a while then."

"Friends—" She thought on that word for a moment. "No. I wouldn't say we have been friends for a long time. When we were teenagers, we tolerated each other, but that was about as close to being friends as we were going to get. We lived next door to each other, rode the same bus, and went to the same school, so our lives just kind of became intertwined by default. At some point during high school, we began to realize that the other had some very useful talents. We realized that, if we were to team up, we could start to do some amazing things."

"You're super smart. That's obviously your main talent. What did he bring to the table that benefited you so much?"

"Z has a way of being able to get things done. People just do things for him. If he wants something, he can get his hands on it. Always. For me, even when I was in high school, I began to have these grand ideas for things I could create, or develop, or invent. None of those things are free."

"So ... his family is rich," I guessed.

"Not even a little bit. He has a lot now because of how he has used his skills over the years to get money, but he comes from nothing. He literally comes from nothing. The house next door—the one he moved into when he was twelve—that was a foster home. It was a two-bedroom place with the exact same floor plan as my house, coming in at just over 1,200 square feet. I remember going over to meet them when they were brand new to the neighborhood. He and his brother kept talking like their new house was a palace."

"Wouldn't you say you two are friends now, though? Or is your relationship still pretty much all business?"

"We're friends now. Sure." She smiled. "He grew on me after a while. We have been through so much together. We have built so much together. It's like he is my brother. We don't get to pick our siblings, and you can't help but love them even though they drive you nuts a lot of the time." She clapped her hands together and then began popping her knuckles. "Okay, that's enough talk. I'm ready to drive this thing!"

I pulled out onto the side of the main road and turned off the engine but left the keys in the ignition. We switched seats.

"Buckle up." Subi laughed. "Waking up in our own beds after dying in Olinc is still just a theory." She turned the key, which caused the truck to lurch forward. The engine died before it could get going.

"You can't just turn the key." I laughed. "You have to start by pushing in the clutch."

Over the next two hours, we spent most of the time practicing with the clutch. Getting the engine going was easy enough, but getting it into gear was a whole different challenge. By the time we decided to call it quits for the day, she could successfully get up to speed, but every time she tried to shift into a new gear, for some reason she would pull the steering wheel to the left as she concentrated her right hand on shifting. It was a good thing there was no oncoming traffic.

"Answer a question for me," I said at one point. "Why aren't there any other cars inside Olinc? I get that there aren't extra people in the system, but why aren't there any cars?"

"There are some cars." She eased off the gas and stepped on the clutch before shifting to a new gear. "If someone were to map out a car sales lot where the cars just sit there indefinitely, then you would find the lot stocked full of cars. Of course, someone like you with the mapping chip would need to add it to Olinc first."

"It would be just like the grocery store, but it would be a Volkswagen in stock instead of a box of raisin bran."

"Exactly. But in the parking lot at the grocery store, or here alongside the roads in Olinc, there are no cars because the system doesn't include things that are constantly changing."

"What would happen if there was one specific car that was always parked in the same parking spot at Walmart every time I went there."

"If it was there consistently enough, then yes." She gripped the steering wheel as she made a turn. "Olinc would expect it to be there, so you would find that car in the parking lot at Walmart even if you were inside Olinc."

We found a large parking lot where Subi felt confident she could turn around, and she was able to drive all the way back to the lighthouse without killing the engine even once. We never made it out of second gear, of course, and the speedometer didn't pass twenty-five miles per hour, but we both considered it a great success.

"Keep going," I said. "The farthest I have explored out there in the real world is just down the road. I'd like to see what the edge of Olinc looks like."

"Okay. It's not really all that interesting, but if you want to see it—"

We drove another five minutes down the road. The farther we were away from the lighthouse, the more the trees and rocks and buildings looked pixelated. By the time we were miles away, everything looked like we were in an 8-bit video game, like we were Mario running around in his first NES Nintendo game.

And then the details just stopped altogether. Everything was white. She drove right into the whiteness. It was unnerving, a lot like trying to drive though the thickest fog. I could feel the sensation of moving, but I saw nothing but white in front of us and to either side.

She pulled the steering wheel to the left and I felt my body shift to one side as we turned. Sections of the world came back into view once we had turned around, and she headed back toward the areas where there were colors and details.

"Not really all that interesting, you said?" I said shaking my head. "That was wild!"

"I guess I've seen it so many times that it's not that exciting to me. When the system was new, before I figured out a good way to streamline the data, it took nearly a year before Olinc was more than just the area right around the hotel."

We drove back toward the lighthouse and found June waiting patiently on the curb. She had her hoodie pulled up around her head and looked like a little schoolgirl with it tied tightly around her chin.

"Let's do that again tomorrow," Subi said after slowing to a stop.

As June was walking across the front of the truck, it suddenly lurched forward at her, and the engine died. June let out a small scream as the pickup jumped toward her before it died.

"What just happened?!" Subi shouted. "I almost killed my friend!"

"She would have been fine ... in theory," I corrected her.

She looked at me in surprise before her lips curled up into a smile. "Seriously, what just happened?"

"You let off the clutch and brake while the engine was still running. If you do that while you're still in gear, it's gonna jerk and die every time."

She shook her head. "Too many things to think about at once."

I opened the passenger side door and stepped out so I could walk around to the driver's side. Subi slid over one spot, which put her in the middle for the drive home.

"How did it go?" June asked with a smile as she shut the passenger door and reached for her seatbelt. "Hopefully you did better overall than that last two minutes."

"I may not have my blackbelt in driving a stick yet, but I at least earned my white belt today," Subi said. She looked at me for confirmation.

"You did great. Tomorrow it's supposed to rain pretty hard, so we'll see how you do in the rain," I said.

Back at the hotel, June stepped out of the pickup. She pulled her clicker out of the pocket, pushed the button, and completely disappeared.

"I was wondering," I said. "I tend to walk all the way back to my room before I click the button. What would happen if we were all to hit our clickers from the lighthouse rather than drive half an hour all the way back home?"

"We would get home just fine. We would appear right back in our rooms, but your truck would still be in Newport by the lighthouse."

"The truck would stay right where I left it? Interesting." I pondered this thought for a moment as I tried to wrap my head around the concept. "Why isn't it like the gallon of milk in the store? You once said that if I'm inside Olinc and I take some milk off the shelf, then the shelf would remain empty until someone in the real world with the mapping chip looked at things and updated the data. I have the mapping chip in my head, so why couldn't we all just click out of Olinc from far away and leave my truck there by the lighthouse? And then as soon as we were back at the hotel in the real world, I could see my truck in the parking lot, and then inside Olinc it would automatically appear back at the hotel."

"For the same reason someone couldn't do that with your body." Subi looked up at the sky and laughed as she was remembering a funny memory from her past. "When the system was new and we were still working out the kinks, everything worked that way, just like you are saying. In those days, if you were walking around inside Olinc and June were to see your body in the real world, then you would teleport inside Olinc right back to your bed where she sees you. And since your real body was lying there motionless in the real world—"

"Then the person plugged into Olinc would have been stuck in that position like a statue," I surmised.

"That only happened once." She began laughing so hard that a tear formed in her left eye. "Ramsey was the only person inside Olinc as we were all in the room experimenting with things. Since June was one of those in the room and she could see his body the whole time, none of us realized he was stuck in there. I still remember him huffing and puffing and whining once he finally got out, saying things like, 'I felt like I was in a coma where my body didn't work but my brain was still fully functional.' He was frozen inside Olinc for over an hour before June stepped out of the room, leaving him finally free to move and able to get to his clicker."

"So, you altered the programming so that couldn't happen anymore, and cars work the same way?"

"Yep. People, cars, June's wheelchair. Anything that would be really bad if it were to suddenly disappear while it was being used. I made a copy of all those things. They look and work just the same, but they're completely independent from the items in the real world."

"June's wheelchair? But I thought—" I began to ask why she would even need a wheelchair inside Olinc, but then I remembered that she hadn't been able to walk until I arrived here. "You say those things are completely independent. What happens if my pickup gets a flat tire in the real world?"

"The truck inside Olinc would be just fine. No flat tire. And if it were to happen the other way around and your truck inside Olinc were to get a flat tire, then your truck would have to stay that way until you replaced the tire inside Olinc. It wouldn't automatically replace itself like the milk at the grocery store because the truck is completely disconnected from anything in the real world. Do you understand?"

"I ... think so."

"Either way, it doesn't matter if you understand how it works. All that matters is that you know your truck is always going to remain exactly where you last left it inside Olinc." She smiled. "So, don't leave the windows down, because it'll probably rain before you drive it again."

"It's weird to think that life goes on inside Olinc even if nobody is in there."

Subi sat motionless and looked at me for a moment. Her demeanor changed just a bit, making me think she had begun thinking of something completely different than what we were talking about.

"What? What is it?" I asked.

She smiled. "You're a good guy, Miles. I think it's time you start attending the group meetings. I think you may have more to offer than just collecting data."

"You don't want me spending my time collecting data anymore?" I was a bit confused. What did I have to offer the team other than data collection? I was no genius.

"We still need you to collect data," she said. "But come to the main lobby at ten o'clock tomorrow morning."

NINE

I wrapped myself up tightly in a thick blanket and sat on my balcony to watch the waves. High tide was such that the water was close enough to reach the concrete barrier directly beneath me when the larger waves came in. From this height, as I looked out from my balcony at a slight angle, I couldn't even see the sand below, which made me feel like I was sitting atop the ocean.

An hour ago, when I had first sat down, there had been a large log resting on the sand just out of the reach of the waves. It mesmerized me to watch the water creep closer and closer to the log, enveloping it on occasion, and successfully moving it a foot or two. Little by little, the water had managed to grab it and pull it back toward the ocean. Now that the waves had the ability to come higher, and now that the log had inched closer and closer to the depths of the ocean, one large group of waves converged to grab hold of it to carry it away.

But the log couldn't float away like a lazy log being carried downstream. Instead, the large piece of drifting wood would tumble and turn like it wanted to either reach dry land or be carried out to sea but wasn't allowed to do either. A new set of waves would come, and the log would just spin and spin without going anywhere.

That was exactly how I was beginning to feel. Up until tonight, everything about this place had made me feel like I was in some sort of dream. Everyone's generosity and friendliness had felt like a wonderful stroke of luck that not only saved me from the county jail but also seemed to give me a new chapter of life where I could be proud of being part of something.

Every time I explored some new area, it would bring me a lot of joy to know I was giving June a new place to stretch her legs. Few things in life could compare to bringing happiness to someone like her, but the words spoken to me by Amos were starting to sit heavily on my mind tonight. Tonight wasn't the first moment they had done so, but they brought me to a whole new level of anxiety as I watched that log twist and turn in the water.

Most specifically, I was beginning to struggle with Subi. Who was she? If I had just awakened here in Lincoln City with zero knowledge of her at all, I would have been excited to spend time around her. She was a lot of fun. Always bright. Always cheerful. She had an intellect that put me in awe every time she talked, and yet, she had a way of still making me feel like I was somehow her equal. I knew I wasn't, but she treated me that way anyway, and she did so in a way that I had no insecurities about it.

And that was what bothered me so much. The problem was that I had indeed met her when I was back in Idaho, and when we had met, she was wearing a wedding ring at the time. For a little while, I started to question whether I had actually seen a ring on her finger, but then I remembered Jason making a big deal out of it. He teased her about being some perfect young mom with a perfect family, or something like that, and I remembered looking at her wedding ring as he was saying those things.

Why did Subi never mention her family? Did she have a bunch of kids back in Idaho? Why was she wearing a diamond on that finger before, but ever since we got here to Oregon, she hadn't worn it even once? That unsettled me.

I had just spent a fun evening with her, teaching her to drive as we bantered back and forth. It made me forget for a moment that she was off the market. I began to feel a spark of something every time she let out a laugh, or the cute way she would grow wide-eyed and bite her bottom lip when she was concentrating extra hard.

I felt like a monster for even beginning to develop feelings toward her. I knew she wasn't available, and yet, I found that I was allowing myself to feel a certain way about her. That was out of the question. I had never cheated on someone before, and I never would. To allow someone so perfect as Subi to do something like that would be even worse on my soul. This was all out of the question.

So why were there moments when it felt like she was flirting with me? I couldn't shake Amos from my mind as I asked myself this question. I could see him in my mind's eye, puffing on a newly lit cigarette and saying, "She wants something from you. She is charming you for a reason, and she is keeping you in the dark."

It made me feel like such a fool. And yet, this was Subi. She wasn't like that, was she? She didn't seem to have a manipulative bone in her body.

I felt restless in my bed that night. When I awakened the next morning, I instinctively went to the sliding glass door and pulled open the curtains to look out across the beach. The log was still there in the same spot. The only difference was that it was now stuck in the sand at a different angle than when I had last seen it. It must have twisted and turned for most of the night until the water finally receded and let it be.

Since I had a few hours before I was supposed to attend a meeting with Subi and Z, I went for a walk along the water.

I didn't make it very far before I noticed Amos again sitting on the railing of his balcony. I had only spoken with him on one occasion, and every second in his presence was like standing out in the cold rain without a jacket, but something drew me to him.

The stairs felt like they were taller than usual, and there were twice as many of them.

I knocked.

"Who's there?" I heard his voice muffled through the door.

"Miles."

There was no response for a long time, and after what was probably a full minute, I contemplated whether to just walk away. Coming to his room had been a bad idea anyway.

But then the door opened, and Amos stood there in front of me, his cigarette hanging from his lips as he tucked a button-up shirt into his jeans. He said nothing as he left the door open and walked back across his room toward the balcony.

I wasn't 100% confident he was giving me permission to enter, but I slowly followed in after him anyway.

"I was just wondering," I said. "Why is it you sit on the balcony like that?" When he continued through the open balcony door without saying a word, the silence got to me and I added, "I mean, surely you know it's dangerous to sit like that. A big gust of wind, or leaning too far one way or something, and ... and that rail can't be comfortable on your butt. I mean, my butt would fall asleep after two minutes of sitting on a rail that thin."

Amos stepped up onto his chair, swung a leg over the railing, and perched on it like before. He took a drag from his cigarette and blew the smoke out through his nose.

"One big gust of wind, or if I am leaning the wrong way, and *splat*!" He clapped his hands together, which made me jump, especially because it meant he had taken both hands off the railing to do so. "I have spent the last years of my life under the thumb of other people. Everyone is always saying, 'This is your prison cell and your bunk, Amos. This is your roommate now, Amos. Lights out, Amos. Here is your lunch, Amos. No, you do not get to choose what you eat, or where you sleep, or your cellmate, Amos.'" He turned his head halfway toward me. "Up here on my balcony, I am the only one in charge. You think you're free as you run around town, but you're not. You are still locked up inside your head."

"I've got my car keys. They even gave me a credit card."

Amos coughed out a deep laugh. "Do you think you are free to drive away? Have you tried asking them yet if you can drive home to Idaho for a weekend?"

I hesitated. I hadn't exactly asked them if I could, but I had offered to make the drive. Subi shot the idea down.

"Up here, I am sitting an inch away from death. I am in complete control. Me." He pointed a finger at his own chest. "An inch from death but not being dead. That is the only time I feel alive."

He pressed the end of his cigarette into the railing. I expected him to drop the butt onto the balcony, or even off the edge, but he didn't. He rolled it in his fingers to squish out any excess tobacco and then slid the butt into his breast pocket.

"Contrast," I said.

"What?"

"Contrast," I repeated. "You need to feel the contrast between life and death in order to feel the life. You need to be able to touch both."

He took a deep, raspy breath. "Yeah. You get it."

"Who is Subi?" I blurted out. "What's her story?"

Amos lifted his leg back over the rail and spun toward me. He still sat in a dangerous way, but at least both legs were on this side now. I hadn't realized I was clutching a fistful of my own T-shirt until his new positioning caused me to relax a bit and I let go.

He nodded. "Subi—she is nice. She is always nice. Maybe that's why I know I can't trust her."

"That doesn't make any sense."

"It does," he shot back. "Do you think she just has a habit of going to the county jail every day to talk them into letting prisoners out just because she is nice? No. The jail would never let anybody out just because she is nice. She had never met you before that day. She knew nothing at all about you. You were a complete stranger to her, and yet, she did you that huge favor. The reason she wanted to let you out, and the reason she was able to do so, was because you have something she wants. That, and because she was willing to give the jail something big in exchange for you. If that doesn't seem nefarious to you, then you're more blind than I am."

"But what?" We had gone through this round before, and ever since our last discussion I couldn't think of anything significant they could want from me. "What would she possibly want from me? I don't have anything to offer."

"You're a lab rat. You're going to end up losing your mind in the end. That's my guess. And then once your brain is mush, they will have no use for you, and they will toss you out with yesterday's garbage."

"I think you're wrong." I was a bit surprised at my own straightforwardness. "I think some people are just nice. I think she's just nice."

He didn't seem even the slightest bit taken aback by my response. "Yeah. I knew you were a fool. You're a sucker for a pretty face."

"I—" I was about to object to his judgement of me, but my mind got stuck on how he referred to her as "a pretty face."

"What, boy? You don't think I can recognize a pretty face just because I'm blind? I know she's pretty because I hear how men talk to her. I hear how men change their behavior and tone when she walks into the room, and they don't do that when June comes in. She is clearly very pretty, and she's very nice. Being pretty and being nice are her best tools to get whatever she wants. She is dangerous. Very, very dangerous."

"I think you're wrong," I said again, and I stood up to walk out.

"You may be a fool for a pretty face, but you're not dumb," Amos said as I walked away. "Just keep in mind what I say. Draw your lines and don't let them force you anywhere you don't want to go. Draw your lines."

I thought he was wrong, and yet, I knew he was right. I needed to draw some lines. What lines? It was a bit difficult to even know where I should consider drawing lines if they still hadn't asked a lot of me yet. Fixing my truck, handing me the keys, and giving me a credit card was hardly the prison sentence Amos was making this out to be. He was crazy, right?

I wondered if this 10:00 meeting I was about to attend was going to change that thinking. Maybe this would be the first time they asked something of me that would make me question their motives. Maybe this would be the moment they would reveal their hand as to why they would pull me, a perfect stranger, out of the county jail to give me a cushy life.

TEN

I thought I was entering the main lobby ten minutes early to my meeting, but when I opened the door, I found that there were already a dozen people sitting around the large oval table.

Subi jumped to her feet when she saw me come in. "Everyone, this is Miles!" She waved for me to come join them.

The only two faces I recognized were those of Z and Subi.

Z sat at the head of the table holding a tablet in one hand, and a writing stylus in the other. Subi was situated at the middle of the table directly across from the only seat unoccupied.

I quietly pulled back the chair and tried not to draw attention to myself as I sat.

Right off the bat I knew something was unusual about all these people. There was a man sitting right next to me with a regular old ballpoint pen in his hand. As he listened to Z talk about something I couldn't understand, he was taking notes. Except, there was no paper on the table in front of him. Whenever he lowered his pen to write, the tip of it disappeared about half an inch below the surface of the table.

A moment later, a young lady stood up and stepped away from the table. Once she was a few steps away from her chair, she disappeared completely for about twenty seconds, and when she reappeared to take her seat again, she was holding a bottle of water in her hand.

Now I was curious. Obviously, none of these people were physically in the room. When the man next to me paused from writing on his invisible piece of paper, I leaned over as if to scratch my leg. I deliberately bumped my elbow into his side to see what would happen. My elbow went right through him like he was a ghost. I felt nothing.

"Tim, would you slap Miles for me?" Z said abruptly.

I looked up, a bit taken aback by his words. The man next to me, who had been taking notes, shifted in his seat, brought a hand back and slapped me right across the face. I flinched back, bringing both forearms up too late to block anything coming my way. Again, I felt nothing as his hand went right through me.

"Sorry about that." Z laughed. "I saw you elbowing Tim and realized you didn't know how any of this works. This is just a conference call."

I had to gather my breath for a second before speaking. "I've never been in a conference call like this. How does it work?" I asked, not quite sure if I was out of line disrupting their meeting by putting the focus back on me.

"It's not all that complicated," Subi said. "It's just like any video conference call you've seen a million times before, except that our system has the ability to do it in 3D."

Next to me, Tim took off his glasses and pointed at them. "We can all see into the conference call when we have these on."

I looked around the room and realized everyone else was also wearing glasses, all with different styles and colors, except for Subi and Z. I assumed they didn't need to wear glasses for the same reason I could see everyone without them.

"I guess I don't need glasses because of this." I rubbed my hand over the round lump behind my left ear.

"That's right," Z said. "And I think that's a good transition point. Let's move on to why Miles is here with us today."

"Miles," Subi said. "We have been really pleased with your progress in the program."

Subi continued to talk for a moment about how they were happy with how things were going with me, but my attention was stuck on her use of the word "progress." What did she mean by that? What "progress" was I making? At first, I thought she must have been talking about the progress I was making with my efforts to build the world of Olinc, but that wasn't it. She was talking as if she still thought of me as someone they had rescued from the county jail who was benefitting from my time in Lincoln City. Why was she talking like this? She knew I wasn't a troublemaker.

Then again, maybe she needed to say these things for the benefit of other people in the room. Perhaps there were people sitting around this table who needed to be convinced I was being reformed by this experimental program. Maybe someone in this room was law enforcement. Or maybe they were even holding the purse strings of the whole operation.

"We want to take you to the next level," Z said. "We want you to continue to grow the world inside Olinc, but your new homework assignment is to come up with something that is completely your own fresh idea. Something you can build, and be proud of, and develop. You have a whole team of geniuses at your disposal to make it happen. Take advantage of that."

"You want me to come up with something useful to do with Olinc?" I asked.

Z placed both hands on the table and leaned in. "It doesn't have to have anything to do with Olinc. It can be anything at all. Invent something. Build something. Start a new business. Anything. We took you out of the jail system so we could use our team to help make a difference in someone's life—a lot more than locking you up could do. We want you to have something you can be proud of. It'll help you work on yourself."

I expected this from Z. I had tried to speak to him on multiple occasions about how I wasn't really a menace to society, and each time he would just nod in obvious disbelief. As he spoke, though, I expected to see something different in Subi's eyes. I was convinced she knew differently.

Subi was taking notes by typing into a tablet. It wasn't until this moment that I realized she was again wearing her wedding ring.

This frustrated me more than it probably should have. Who was I to judge whether she should wear her wedding ring? A lot of people take theirs on and off throughout the day when they do certain activities, or even just at times when they don't feel like wearing it.

This confused me, though. She had seemed a bit flirtatious the evening before when I was teaching her to drive my truck. Was this all part of the program? Was it all an act? A game she was playing to help me "progress?"

"So, why don't you tell the whole team what you think of Olinc so far," Subi said, snapping me out of my reverie.

There was something in the way she spoke to me that amplified my frustration. We had spoken countless times over the past few months, and she had always looked me in the eye. She had always spoken to me like a friend. But today, here in this formal meeting with that ring on her finger, she talked to me like I was just some random person off the street they invited into their meeting. The connection I typically felt when we made eye contact was absent.

I looked around at all the curious faces. When I spoke, I didn't do a very good job at masking the aggravation I was feeling in the moment. "It's okay, I guess."

"Just okay?" One man scoffed.

My frustration level came down a notch as I thought about June. "When I'm with June, Olinc is one of the most amazing things I have ever seen in my entire life. She is a real treasure of a human being, and it brings me a lot of joy to see how well it works for her. She can walk. She loves to skip around like she's a six-year-old child on a playground. It's a beautiful thing."

"But ...?" Subi asked, looking curious about where this was going to go.

"I don't see how this is going to be very practical for most people," I said. "I don't know how it all works, but I'm sure it costs a fortune to create this system and keep it running." I pointed to the implant behind my ear. "I had to be asleep for a week to have this thing implanted in me, and I'm still not sure what it even is. That's not very practical. Not very many people are going to be willing to let you implant something into their brain. It's crazy when you think about it. It took a team of surgeons to do it. Who is going to have the money to do something like that?"

"That's fair," Z said. "But you let us worry about the funding. I get the feeling that's not really what bothers you."

I took a breath and looked down at my hands on the table for a moment as I pondered. "Being inside Olinc is ... empty." I lifted my head and looked around the table. "There's nobody in there. That's all fine and great for someone like June who wants to meditate as she overlooks the ocean, but for the rest of us ... to me it feels lonely. It feels like the rapture has already happened."

The room was silent. It felt obvious they were expecting my first report to be a lot more complimentary of all their hard work.

I knew that my frustration was making me bolder than was my norm, and it was pushing me to say things I didn't mean. I knew the words coming out of my mouth were a lie even as I was saying them. I knew Olinc was a special place.

For people like June, the gift of being able to walk again was one that gave her a whole new level of joy in her life. She wasn't just in a different world when she was inside Olinc, she was on top of the world.

I could also see the potential in replacing parts of the judiciary and prison system with this, if that were really a possibility. It needed better planning and a lot of work, but it was easy to see the potential there.

I knew Olinc was a nice respite from the busy beehive of the real world. I could easily see a rich businessman who lived in the high-rises of Manhattan wanting to have a chip implanted in him so he could disconnect from the hustle and bustle of city life, whether for a few hours or a few days, and take a vacation without ever leaving the confines of his bedroom.

On the other hand, while I felt Olinc was a valuable and priceless idea, the distrust I was feeling toward everyone in this room was growing. Before this meeting, although I felt wary about Z, I felt like Subi deserved all my loyalty. Now, with the change in the way she was looking at me, even she made me wonder if she was using me in a way I couldn't understand.

Everything I was feeling inside centered around my growing distrust, whether I knew everyone personally or not.

"You're asking a lot of people to trust you in a big way by letting you implant something into their head. Just the thought of that—" I said. "I mean, there's a reason you started with someone like me. I was desperate to get out of my situation at the county jail, and you knew it. I don't want to say you took advantage of me, because I came here willingly, but I can't see a lot of people being so keen to let you implant them with something into their brain. That's the way a lot of sci-fi horror stories begin."

"He's not wrong," a woman said from the end of the table.

The room remained quiet for a moment as everyone pondered my words.

"You said you see the beauty in what Olinc has done for June," Subi said calmly.

"I do," I said.

"Let's work with that," she said. "Even if those are the only people we are able to touch for a long time, until we can figure out more practical ways of using Olinc to benefit the world, let's focus on that."

"Miles," Z said. "We want to ask something of you."

Here we go. I could tell by the tone in his voice that this was important to him, which didn't exactly make me want to trust him more.

"I have seen you up on the top floor talking to Amos," Z said. "Do you have a rapport with him?"

"Not really," I said.

"Will you work on that?" Subi asked. "Will you get him to trust you? You're a good guy. Easy to trust."

"Why do you need me to have rapport with him?" I asked.

"We want him to be part of this," Z said. "Like you pointed out, it's not exactly easy to get people to allow us to put an implant in them. He has one, but he refuses to use it. We would like you to see if you can get him to plug into Olinc. We think he could really benefit from it."

I couldn't argue with that. Watching June inside Olinc was the best part of any of this. Amos was hardly the life of the party, but there was something about him that did make me want the best for him.

"Yeah," I said calmly. "I'll see what I can do."

ELEVEN

I went straight from the meeting back to my room to reflect. At first, I found myself thinking about how I could get Amos to connect himself to Olinc, or even if I wanted to, and then about what kind of idea I could come up with to have something of my own—everything we had discussed in the meeting.

Then I realized how much of my mental space was being taken up by things other people wanted me to do. I wanted to do something for myself for a change. I wanted to think about me. I wanted to indulge in spoiling myself with something that was fun for me. Me. Me. Me.

The problem was that as I grabbed my keys and jumped in my truck, there wasn't anywhere I wanted to go, so I just began driving around Lincoln City. I drove through the center of town looking for anything that might catch my attention.

There was some place called Christmas Cottage that I had seen each time I drove through town where, apparently, it was Christmas every day of the year and anyone could come buy Christmas trinkets. That wasn't the least bit interesting to me.

A candy shop that looked like it specialized in saltwater taffy was more tempting than Christmas ornaments this time of year, but I have never been a real candy lover. That wasn't me, so I just kept driving.

When I made it all the way through town and found myself driving through the woods, I flipped back around and ran through the list I had created in my head. There wasn't a whole lot to see in Lincoln City, Oregon, which was probably why they chose this as the central location of their experiment in the first place. It was a simple little town. It was beautiful without the need for exciting amusement parks or other attractions. It was charming without the need for flash.

I found myself focusing on two stops that had caught my attention the first time through town. I resisted at first, telling myself this whole selfish quest was dumb in the first place, and I should just go find some new place to explore, but I made the two stops anyway.

Back in my truck, I couldn't help but shake my head and laugh at myself. I set out on a mission to do something selfish, and the two things I ended up buying were a fancy kite from the fancy kite store, and an ice cream cone. What was wrong with me? I had the ability to squander money on anything I could possibly want. If anyone were to look at my bank statement, they would probably wonder if a six-year-old kid had stolen my credit card for the afternoon.

As silly as I felt making those two purchases, though, I quickly found that I had made the right choice. I hadn't flown a kite since I was about eight years old, and that was a cheap piece of plastic with SpongeBob SquarePants printed on it. I had been able to get that thing hovering in the air for less than five minutes before it smashed down to the earth, snapping its thin wooden frame, and rendering it completely useless.

I rather hated the wind on most days. It was not nearly as irritating as getting rained on, but I still didn't like it. Living in Lincoln City, I didn't usually have a choice on either one. It was almost always windy and raining to some degree. But today felt different. The sun was out, and the wind on my back was a welcome feeling as it kept the tension on my string. I stared up at the heavens, watching my kite sway from side to side as the gusts kept my string taut.

My cell phone chimed in my pocket. I knew who it was, and I knew why she was reaching out to me, but she could wait a few minutes for a response. My answer would be yes, I would be happy to take Subi out for another driving lesson in the evening, but right now I was busy.

"Where do we want to go today?" I asked the two ladies once we were all inside Olinc.

"Wherever you two want to go," June said.

"We are going to practice driving again," Subi said. "So, our location doesn't really matter to us. You pick."

"In that case, let's just go back to the lighthouse," June said. "I could seriously go there every day."

We pulled up to the same place as yesterday. I kept the truck idling as June stepped out, expecting that we would just be dropping her off and heading right back out to the main road, but Subi changed her mind.

"You know what?" Subi said, "I was watching the migration reports this morning of the gray whales. They are expected to come through here today. Let's go down and sit on the beach for a while to see if they come."

I was game for that. I had been able to spot them a few times as I was exploring beaches, and their majestic beauty made my heart skip a beat every time one came into view.

June assumed her usual spot near the lighthouse overlooking the ocean. Subi and I walked down a small trail and descended the side of the cliff by means of some manmade stairs. We ended up at one of my favorite locations in the whole area. I loved it so much that I had spent more time than usual here. My extra attention to detail paid off as we found a comfortable spot on a log to sit and soak it all in.

Cobble Beach was a fascinating place. Mother Nature must have spent countless millennia crafting this beautiful little spot. The floor of this beach, located at the base of a set of breathtaking cliffs, had no dirt or sand. It was completely made up of jet-black cobblestones, all of which were roughly the size of chicken eggs.

Dozens of seals enjoyed sunbathing on the large rock formations out in the water. They would take turns getting curious about us humans and would periodically slip into the water to come get a closer look at us.

"How does this work?" I asked. "I know the answer is probably going to go right over my head, but how does it work with animals inside Olinc? They're not really here, right?" I pointed at a seal about forty feet from us with its head bobbing just above the water. "I mean, if we were out in the real world, there wouldn't be a seal right there watching us, would there?"

"The artificial intelligence part of the system does most of the work with that, but there is also a small team that works on just that—only that," Subi said. "I love animals. They fascinate me, and make me laugh, and make me marvel, and ... they're just so beautiful. To me, they're a crucial part of what makes Olinc special. The team is tasked with knowing how many seals populate this area, and then they connect that information to things like the weather and how that would affect their behavior patterns. You've obviously done a good job watching the way they act and interact with each other, because they seem very natural to me."

"I do love the seals. They're probably my favorite animal out here."

I was trying to ignore the awkward feelings building inside me, but I couldn't shake them. When she looked at me this morning at the meeting, something felt different. Something felt a little off. But now she was relaxed again. I felt comfortable again sitting next to her, which made me wildly more uncomfortable than ever before. My insides were being pulled in two directions.

When I looked down at her left hand and saw that she was not wearing her ring, I blurted out without even considering my words, "Who are you?"

Taken aback, she said nothing, but just looked at me, confused.

I paused before rewording my question. "I mean, I can't quite figure you out. You're pretty flirty, you know that? You're beautiful. You're nice. You're a lot of fun, but ... are you married, or what? One moment you're wearing a wedding ring, and then you're not, and then you are." I pointed down at her left hand. "Right now, you're not."

She looked me in the eye for a long while. Trying my best to read her, it was easy to see this question overwhelmed her.

She picked up a black stone and turned it over in her hands a few times. "It's complicated."

It didn't seem like a complicated question to me, though. Was she married or not? There really was no in between. The silence after her confusing response grew more uncomfortable with each passing second, but I wasn't about to let her off the hook. I needed to know.

"I'm not married," she said simply.

"You're engaged?"

She shook her head. "No. I used to be married, but I'm not married any longer."

I felt that the questions in my head were already obvious, so I didn't voice them. I had forced us into a place where she would either answer them or avoid them. She knew what I wanted to know, and it was up to her whether she would give that to me.

For a long, awkward moment, I assumed she was going to leave my curiosity hanging, but she didn't.

"I got married to my high school sweetheart about a year after high school," she said. "I think I'd rather save the difficult details for another day, but let's just say he began to fall apart about two years after we got married. It was hard to watch. I still loved him, but he was falling apart. Really falling apart. Over the course of another year or so, he wasn't himself anymore." She tossed the black stone underhand into the water. "And then one day he was just gone. He was just gone."

"Gone, as in ... he was a different person?"

"Gone, as in ... I came home from work one day and he was gone. No note. No text message. No phone call. Nothing." She turned her head toward me. Although her eyes were dry, the pain behind them was palpable. "I believe he's out there somewhere. I don't know where. I don't know if he's living alone on the streets, or maybe he is in a mansion somewhere with a new family. I have no idea. I haven't had so much as a text message from him since he left."

A minute ago, I had felt entitled to her answers. I had felt she owed me an explanation. As those answers came, however, those feelings were quickly replaced by a sentiment of invasiveness. With each word she shared, I felt more intrusive. Still, I had to know. "How long ago was that?"

"Three years. Three years since he left. Two years since the divorce was final."

"You said you haven't had any contact. You were able to finalize the divorce without having any contact?"

She nodded. "That's why I'm pretty sure he's out there somewhere. Ramsey has a way of being able to get things done. He had someone find him. He got the divorce taken care of for me without me having to lift a finger. And yet, I won't let Z tell me anything about where he is. I'm not ready to know yet."

"It hurts too much," I said, more of a statement than a question.

"Yes. It hurts too much." She fanned out the fingers on her left hand and held it out in front of us. "Some days I can't let it go. Some days I can't admit that I failed. I failed him. I failed myself. I failed at marriage. I know it doesn't make sense, but some days I still wear my ring because I just can't stomach the idea that it's ..."

When her voice trailed off, I noticed that she had lost the fight to keep her tears at bay.

"Sorry." She wiped her eyes. "I don't know what came over me. It's been a while since I've fallen apart talking about this. I mean, it's been years now. I should be able to talk about it without melting."

"No. There's nothing wrong with letting things hurt sometimes. I'm sorry I stuck my nose where it doesn't belong. I feel bad for pushing."

"You were right to push. I'm sorry for being flirty. I know I come off that way. I don't mean to."

"What is—" I struggled to find the right words. I didn't quite even know what I was trying to say, myself. "What is my role in this? I mean, are we buddies? Am I still just some sort of experiment?"

"This is going to sound really selfish. This is so embarrassing." She stuck her legs out in front of her and put one foot over the other. "Remember back at the jail in Idaho? Remember how I suggested I wanted to bring you along and how Ramsey wanted to bring that other guy, Jason? We've talked about how Ramsey gets all excited about the idea of transforming someone from crook into saint. Well, I think that's all fine for him. I don't have anything against that idea. I don't have anything against that experiment, but it's not nearly as important to me as it is to him." She paused and scratched nervously at the back of her neck as if she was trying to figure out how to say what was coming next. "But for me? I needed a friend." She slapped both hands over her face. "That makes me sound so pathetic."

"It doesn't, actually." I sat next to her on the log. "It tells me how loyal you were to your husband. It makes me think you gave your whole life to your home, and when that got yanked out from beneath you ... a person can only go so long without having someone to share life with."

She pulled her hands down from her face. "I got lucky with you. If we had come to the jail one day earlier, you wouldn't have been there. I have June and Z here in Oregon, but June is more like a mother figure than a friend, and Z is ... well, he's just Z. And now, here I am like a silly little schoolgirl passing you a note in class asking if you will be my friend."

"Check yes or no?" I said with a laugh.

She let out a small chuckle. "Please be my friend. Please be my friend," she said in a childlike voice. "I'm so pathetic."

"You're not, though."

Without even thinking about it, I placed one arm around her. I felt her stiffen up for just a moment, but then she relaxed and leaned in. For the longest time, we sat there on that log with my one arm around her shoulder as we both looked out across the water. We both gasped at the same moment when the back of a gray whale came into view as it breached the surface about fifty yards away.

She leaned in a little closer and rested her head on my shoulder.

As I sat there, not daring to move even though my butt was beginning to fall asleep from the awkward angle in which I was sitting, she said, "Thanks for being ... you."

TWELVE

The next few months blurred together as my routine completely took over. Each morning, I started the day wrapped in a blanket on my balcony with a hot cup in my hands thinking about where I should work that day. I found myself focusing on one of two criteria with regards to the places I liked to build. I either wanted to give June new places to explore and relax, or I wanted new places to hang out with Subi.

Subi had to spend a lot of her time working. Whenever I stopped by her house to see how she was doing, she was always sitting at her computer. She had four large monitors situated around her working desk, and I gave up early on trying to make sense of anything that appeared on them. She was the mastermind behind Olinc, and whatever she was doing, or inventing, or experimenting with on her fancy-schmancy computer system, it was all lost on my simple mind.

Things changed a little bit for us after we'd had our talk down on Cobble Beach. As the months went by, she let her guard down a little more. Whether I stopped by her place first thing in the morning, late at night, or anywhere in between, she always dropped what she was doing the second I walked in the door. Above all, she was always as happy to see me as I was to see her.

I passed the little Bijou Theater one afternoon as I was driving through town, and a lightbulb lit up over my head. It was the most adorable little movie theater that dated back to the 1930s. I spent two days walking every inch of it between showtimes, both inside and out, and presented Subi with my idea once I had mapped it all out. She was just as excited as I was and said she would get to work immediately on making it work.

Three days later she texted me to inform me she had successfully linked my Bijou Theater data to her own online movie streaming account, and that evening we were going to have the theater to ourselves inside Olinc. For our first personal showing, we wanted to invite as many people as possible, but there were only three other people we could invite. June would most likely be happy to come no matter what flick we were showing. Z would probably come if we let him be the one to pick the movie.

And then there was Amos. There was pretty much no chance he was ever going to want to come to something like that. I visited him on occasion but could never get him to leave his room. His life consisted almost solely of going from one cigarette to the next. Sometimes he was listening to the television or an audiobook when I stopped by. Oftentimes he was just sitting there on his balcony railing—right on the edge "between living and dying," as he would say.

I felt embarrassed every time I sat in on one of the Olinc team meetings. My updates were always the same—I was still working on building a rapport with Amos, but I was not getting very far. He wasn't interested in anything Olinc had to offer him. Not even a little bit.

Everything changed one day when I asked Z a simple question. "People say you have the ability to nudge others into doing things you'd like them to do," I said. "What's the secret?"

A lot of people would have taken my question as a bit of an insult. I know that I sure would have since I was essentially telling him he was manipulative, but Z looked at me like I had just given him the highest compliment he had ever received.

"You have to speak their language," he said. "If someone speaks only German, and you speak only Japanese, you're not going to get very far. You have to learn to speak German first."

I looked at him a bit confused before his reasoning clicked. "Everyone has their own way of thinking. Their own way of communicating. I need to learn to speak Amos."

Z pointed a finger at me as if to say, "You got it."

That simple conversation sent my mind on a whole new path. With every conversation we had, I was speaking to him in Miles, and he was speaking back to me in Amos. That conversation wasn't going anywhere.

Being in Lincoln City and helping with Olinc had rewired my brain. I found that I did some of my best thinking and pondering as I just walked and walked, especially if I walked along one of the beaches.

I drove up north to the Neskowin area and walked the beach there. It was low tide, so I had access to some of my favorite spots.

As I walked, I dissected every bit of every conversation I could recall having with Amos. He was as stubborn as they came. How could I reason with someone whose favorite thing in the world was to know someone wanted something from him, and he had the power to not give it? As long as he had that power, he was happy. Grumpy and miserable ... but happy in his own way.

Maybe that was it. Perhaps the way to get through to him was to somehow figure out how to convince him he still held all the power in the relationship even if he were to connect himself to Olinc.

One thing I knew for sure was that he didn't respect anyone who was nice. Was that one of my biggest problems? Was that one of the main reasons he didn't budge even a millimeter when I was speaking to him? I wasn't sure I could change anything by attempting to be bullish since that wasn't my native language, but it was worth a try.

What was the worst thing that could happen?

Well, I could completely blow things up and ruin what little bit of a relationship we did have, but what loss would that be? I wasn't getting anywhere with him anyway.

I ran over possible scenarios in my mind on the drive back to Lincoln City and worked hard to build up my nerve.

"You got this. You got this," I said out loud to myself as I climbed the stairs to his room.

"Who is it?" his gruff voice sounded from behind the door.

I truly did wonder why he always asked this whenever I knocked. I had never seen another person ever dare knock on his door, let alone set foot inside his room.

I stepped inside without waiting for him to come open the door.

"Who else would it be?" I said, pretending to be brave.

He smirked without bothering to turn his head toward me. He was sitting in his chair in the corner of the room with his small table in front of him and an ashtray that desperately needed to be emptied.

"You're scared," I said matter-of-factly.

"Excuse me?" His cigarette was dancing up and down between his lips as he spoke.

"You're scared."

"I am not scared of anything."

"You sit up there on your balcony pretending that you're balancing between life and death, but you're not. You think you're tough because you're not scared of death, but the truth is, you're scared of life."

He pulled the cigarette from his mouth and smashed it into the ashtray more forcefully than usual, causing a few of the other butts to pop out onto the table.

"You don't know what you are talking about," he snarled. "Just because I don't want to be someone's puppet does not mean I am scared. I am nobody's puppet. I make the rules for myself. I am the only one. Just me."

"What's your favorite food?"

He looked a bit taken aback by this sudden change in direction, which caused him to pause. I could tell he was trying to navigate where this conversation was about to go, so he could decide if he wanted to participate.

"Why? Do you want to take me out on a date?" He grinned.

"What's your favorite food?"

"Lobster," he said, throwing his hands up in frustration as if to say, "Fine. I'll play your game. I'll answer your stupid question."

"If Z were to come up here to your room and offer you the finest lobster dinner made by the most talented chef in the area, and you knew that the only other thing you had around was a loaf of white bread and some bologna—" I took a few steps closer and sat on the edge of his bed. "If he told you he went out of his way to make all this happen and he really wanted to do something nice for you, I bet you would kick him in the butt as he was walking out your door. And then you would turn around and eat your bologna sandwich with miserable pride."

"Z does not do anything unless he wants something in return. I'm not selling myself for some lousy meal."

"How is it you don't get it? How thick are you? It's like trying to reason with a sheep."

There, I had done it. I had come into the room with the goal of pushing him and insulting him. I knew these weren't exactly the worst insults one man could sling at another, but for me it was pretty good.

"I am no sheep," he muttered under his breath, his teeth clenched.

I could tell he was beginning to fume. I didn't yet know if that was a good or a bad thing, but it was different than any reaction I had gotten from him before, and anything different was worth exploring further.

"Sheep are sheep because they're predictable," I said calmly. "A sheep-dog doesn't get surprised by the sheep's sudden break from routine or cleverness. A few loud barks and a few nips at their heels and they're perfectly predictable."

"Get out of my room," Amos said through his teeth.

"You're scared of life," I said, bringing the conversation full circle. "You just want everything predictable. No risks. No adventure. No living."

"I said get out of my room." His voice was getting louder with each word.

"You refuse to enjoy any part of life because you're afraid it will bring someone else a tiny bit of pleasure. Truth is, if you're experiencing the greater amount of pleasure, then you're holding all the cards. But you're folding no matter what cards you're holding. You're weak."

That did it. He grabbed his table with both hands and flung it halfway across the room. The ashtray smashed against the wall, sending cigarette butts in all directions and breaking into pieces on the floor.

That was definitely my cue to get out of there. I had pushed him as far as I could, and I worried that any more from me would push him to something worse than what he had just done to his table.

I heard his footsteps and his breathing behind me as I made my way to the door. I wanted to be quick about my exit now, but I knew I needed to take my time in order to continue my charade of being a tough guy. I was barely out the door when he slammed it shut behind me.

I took three steps away before turning back around. I opened his door to see he was standing in the center of his room with his hands on both hips. He turned back toward me at the sound of me cracking the door back open.

"You say you're free, but we both know that's a lie," I said. "When was a time you felt free? What's the freest you have ever felt in your life?"

He ignored me and walked out onto his balcony.

I closed the door again and went down the stairs to my own room. My heart was pounding. I had no idea if what I had just done was a good thing or not. I had no idea if what I had done had just gotten the wheels in his mind turning, or if he was going to sneak into my room at night and stab me.

I sat on my balcony and looked out over the water. The air was a lot warmer today than it had been over the last few weeks. I didn't need a blanket yet, probably not until the sun was down.

The sky was clear. The heavy fog that usually hung over the ocean this time of day was not as thick as usual. It had been a while since I had been able to watch the sunset, but I would see it clearly today.

There was a family of four off in the distance, down on the beach below. A boy who looked to be a young teenager was throwing a tennis ball as far as he could and would then wait for their dog to bring it back. Mom and Dad sat side by side in the dry sand.

There was also a young girl, most likely a bit younger than the boy. She had a long stick in her hand, and she was walking around the wet sand as she dragged the stick behind her. She was carving different shapes like hearts and smiley faces into the sand as she went.

This was the moment an interesting idea first came to me. This was the moment I knew what I wanted to present to the team—an idea I could call my own!

Before I could develop the idea too far in my head, though, I heard a knock on my door.

I jumped up from my chair and hurried to answer it. Every once in a while, June would come knocking, but nine times out of ten it would be Subi there.

I opened it with a smile but was quickly surprised by Amos standing there in front of me.

"I was not always blind, you know," he said. "I lost my sight some years back to a degenerative disease that took my eyes."

"I'm sorry to hear that." I realized I had dropped my whole macho, tough-guy routine completely.

"I used to love to ride my motorcycle. It was a custom-made chopper that was so beautiful it made everyone's heads turn everywhere I went. Whether I was parked at the local biker bar, or whether I was stopped somewhere on a long road trip across the country, every biker wanted to get a look at it. I rode the whole country. Oregon. Texas. The Dakotas. Everywhere," he said. "When I was out riding, that was the most freedom I had ever felt. The wind on my heels and the sounds of my wheels ... that was my freedom."

I realized why he was telling me this. "I can get you that again," I said, although I wasn't completely sure I had the permission or the power.

He said nothing but only nodded and walked away.

THIRTEEN

We were scheduled to have another team meeting the next morning, but there was no way I could wait that long to tell someone. I was bubbling over with all kinds of excitement. Finally connecting with Amos helped me feel like I was contributing in a grand way. Sure, I had been constantly working hard on building the geography and the detail inside Olinc, and watching June benefit in so many ways from having new territory was a beautiful sight to see, but I had been feeling like such a failure lately that I felt extremely proud to finally have this specific piece to contribute to the team.

I still didn't know why it was important to have Amos on board. I think if I were leading the team, I would have probably sent him back to jail a long time ago and tried to find someone else. Surely there were other people who could benefit from this experiment just as much, or more, than Amos.

Excited to share my news, I hurried down the stairs and across the parking lot to Subi's house. Like usual, she was sitting at her huge desk, clacking away at her computer keyboard and staring at the four large monitors around her. Also, like usual, she was in a great mood and shared equally in my excitement.

I hadn't known quite what I was promising when I told Amos I could make things happen for him, so I was relieved when Subi informed me regarding how straightforward the process would be. For the most part, all I needed to do was to pick a route and drive it repeatedly. The more I drove a route, the more realistic and detailed it could be.

I wanted to do the best job I could on building this world for Amos, which meant that more data could be gathered for the system if I were to perform the task in the same way Amos would—on a motorcycle rather than in my truck. The wind on my face and the sounds of the road would all make a big difference in stitching together all the details of the full experience. If I were to take the trips on the same Harley that Amos would be using, then details about the bike could all be included.

The next morning, when I stepped out my front door to walk down to the meeting, I found my pickup truck parked in the center of the parking lot with a small trailer attached to the back of it. It took me a second to realize this was a specialized type of trailer meant for hauling a motorcycle. Apparently, the team was wasting no time at all getting this ball rolling, and my assignment for today was obviously going to be for me to come home with a new set of wheels for Amos.

"There's a problem," I said to the team. "I don't have a motorcycle license. I can't legally ride a motorcycle on the roads."

"But you have ridden before, right?" Z asked. "Do you know how to ride a motorcycle?"

"Yes. I've ridden before," I said. "Mostly dirt bikes, but I've ridden street bikes too. I'm not worried about crashing or safety or anything like that."

"Then there's no problem," Z said. "I'll get it arranged."

"Do I need to take a test? A written test? A driving test?" I asked.

"Not if I'm the one asking for it to be done," Z said cooly. "Take Amos with you to the Harley-Davidson dealer in Salem. Let him pick one out. Whichever one he wants. By the time you get home, your new license will be sitting on the nightstand next to your bed."

That surprised me a little. I knew he had the ability to get things done, but this wasn't some shop owner doing him a favor. Granted, this was just the local DMV, but his level of confidence, and the fact that he didn't even have to make a phone call before making a promise, made me wonder just how far up the levels of bureaucracy his influence could go.

"I've got to say—I didn't know if you were going to be able to pull this off," Z said. "Amos has proven to be a very tough nut to crack."

Someone at the other end of the table began to clap, and within seconds the entire room was applauding.

"Well, he still hasn't connected himself to Olinc yet," I said sheepishly. "Let's not count our chickens before they hatch."

Z spoke for only another minute or two, and was about to disband the meeting, but I had one more thing I wanted to bring up. I raised my hand awkwardly, just high enough over my head to catch Z's attention.

"Actually, I've got something." I looked around the table at each person individually. The applause I had just received had felt nice, and I felt validated in my value to the team, but now I was worrying about whether my new idea was going to be shot down immediately upon committee. It wasn't exactly the most groundbreaking invention idea anyone had ever come up with.

"So ... you know how you told me I should come up with something that is my own?" I said. "Something I could design or invent? My own fresh idea?"

"Yeah," Z said excitedly. "You got something?"

"Hopefully you don't all think this is dumb, but I think it would be kind of fun. Kind of cool." I began drawing on the table with my fingertip. "I was watching this kid draw designs in the sand yesterday with a stick. She was having a great time. I've seen people do this many times since I've been here. And I've noticed that when other people walk by, they always take a second to look, and they pretty much always walk around them. Even if it's a silly little drawing that was obviously done by a child, people will go out of their way to walk around them and not mess them up." I looked around the table at each person. I felt like I had their interest, but nobody seemed to know where I was going with this quite yet. "Long story short, I want to have a machine—maybe about the size of a lawnmower—that will make big elaborate designs in the sand. If I design something on the computer that's maybe 200 feet wide or so, and then set some GPS coordinates somehow or whatever ... and then it drags a stick or something to carve into the sand ... and then ..." I closed my eyes and shook my head. "It's a dumb idea, isn't it? Never mind."

"I don't think it's dumb at all," Subi said. "I think it would be really cool to program it to work as the tide is going out so it could finish at low tide. Throughout the day, as high tide rolls in, it would wash it away and give a nice new canvas for another design."

"It would be pretty simple to make," one lady said as she looked up at Z. "If you give us the go-ahead, I bet we could have a prototype made within a few weeks."

"Really? That fast?" I asked, happily surprised that the team wasn't just brushing off my idea.

"Whenever my family comes to the coast for vacation," another man said, "I'm always the first one awake in the morning. Until my family wakes up, I always spend the first hour or so just sitting out on the patio watching the waves. If I were a guest at a place like the Seaside Hotel, I think people would really love to wake up each morning to see what the new design would be."

"I think watching the machine work would be a lot of fun, too," Subi added. "I can see myself just sitting there for an hour as I watch it slowly come together."

* * *

Driving Amos to the Harley-Davidson dealer in Salem was interesting. I had only seen one side of him up to this point, and that was the pessimistic side that talked like he could see through everyone's façade to understand the real, ill-intentioned person beneath it all.

I expected this same Amos to answer the door when I came knocking, but I was pleasantly surprised to find a newly showered and dressed Amos waiting for me on the edge of his bed with the front door already open. His hair was slicked back. He had shaved his typically unkempt beard into a nicely trimmed Fu Manchu mustache.

After an hour on the road, we arrived at the Harley-Davidson dealership. Amos grabbed the back of my elbow as we walked across the parking lot and through the double doors.

"You are going to need to do all the talking," Amos said.

"How come? You're the one picking out the bike. I don't really know much about them."

"Because a motorcycle salesman is not going to understand why a blind man is looking to buy a motorcycle for himself. That's why. He is going to direct all his attention to you, so you should do all the talking. I am not much for chit-chat anyway."

Amos was right. When we were approached by a salesman, he looked right past Amos as if he weren't even there and gave me all his attention. I thought this was a bit rude, but Amos clearly didn't mind. He stood out of the way most of the time.

I listened as the salesman described the specs and details of each motorcycle. When the salesman and I were finished looking over one bike, we would move on to the next one while Amos would take a turn examining the one we had just abandoned. I watched him out of the corner of my eye as he slid his hands over every inch of the beautifully crafted machine. He would periodically pause on different parts of the bike to feel it with his fingertips and to marvel at the craftsmanship.

After the salesman and I had discussed each Harley on the showroom floor, he left us to give us space to think things through. Amos narrowed his decision down to three bikes that were quite different from each other, and then over the course of about fifteen more minutes, he decided upon a charcoal-gray bike with a matte finish. The leatherwork was impeccable.

Personally, I was relieved he chose this one over that which ended up being his second choice. I would need to spend a lot of time on whichever bike he chose, and the other one looked like it rode too far back and too low for my comfort. The one he decided upon was more of a conventional ride.

I didn't know much about the gear we would need, so Amos gave me a list. I picked out two of each—one to fit me, and one in Amos's size.

Being around Amos so much forced my mind to work in different ways than I was accustomed. Although we didn't talk much during the hours we spent in the cab of my pickup truck, I couldn't help but absorb his pessimistic energy. I had been feeling good about the ideas I had previously brought to the group meeting, but with so much time to think as I sat quietly next to him, the gloomier I felt about my contributions. My sand-designing machine wasn't exactly a groundbreaking idea because there were a million GPS guided machines out there. This team was used to brainstorming and carrying out plans that could make lame people walk, make blind men see, and recreate entire worlds of beauty.

As I thought about how pleased they were with my idea, I couldn't help but wonder if they were patronizing me. They didn't seem like they were, but how could it be that they were so willing to share in my excitement about just making a machine that could draw doodles in the sand?

I concluded that the team was still focused on ... me! Did they even care about my idea, or did they just care that I was the one who came up with it? If I had proposed an idea for something completely ridiculous, or something that had already been invented years ago, would they have pretended to be excited about it?

Then again, maybe they actually were interested in it. Maybe my idea would be an enjoyable break from the projects they had been working on. I truly did think it would be fun to come up with new designs to make along the beach. And while it was obviously not the type of thing every family in the country would need or want to own, I thought it would be cool for hotel resorts or large beach events to utilize.

I guessed only time would tell what would come of my idea, and whether the team actually valued it.

FOURTEEN

Even after spending a day building some form of relationship with Amos, he still wasn't the slightest bit interested in joining us at the movies, so we didn't push.

We thought it would be fun for each of us to pick a movie, and we would watch one each night together for the first four nights. The catch was that the movie needed to be one that the other people would never pick on their own.

I chose first, and I selected a movie I hadn't seen in years called *A Talent for the Game*. It was a story about a major league baseball scout whose car broke down in the middle of rural America. He walked to the nearest town and came upon a local baseball game where a young phenom happened to be pitching. Before long, the scout talked the team owner into giving him a contract and he pitched in the major leagues.

We weren't into the movie more than twenty minutes before I was burying my face into my hands with embarrassment. When I was thirteen years old, this was the greatest movie of all time. As a young adult, I found myself rolling my eyes with every ridiculous plot twist and the cringeworthy dialogue.

June picked the movie for the second night, and she chose *The NeverEnding Story*. I had seen this movie once when I was young, and to a seven-year-old boy it felt like a grand adventure that took me on an exciting journey. Now, as I watched it as a grownup, I had myself geared up for a long ride, but the movie was over in less than an hour and a half.

"Did we just watch the edited version or something?" I asked as the closing credits rolled out. "Was that really how long the full movie is?"

Z had originally chosen for us to watch *The Godfather*. I was indifferent to the idea since I had never seen it. Subi protested saying a movie like that sounded terrible, but he wasn't interested in budging. He went on and on about how it was a classic, and how it told such an interesting story of human nature because it was a "perfect study of psychology, mixed with genius cinematography."

It wasn't until June said simply, "That movie would make me uncomfortable," that he changed his mind immediately. We watched *Rocky* instead.

Subi's choice was *Fiddler on the Roof.* Of the four movies we watched, this was the only one I had never seen before. I had a strong aversion to musicals. Every time people would burst out in song, I would get an overwhelming feeling of, "Oh, no. Not again." But this one was different. The music wasn't too bad. The storyline was great. The fact that the movie was so incredibly long was balanced out by the fact that I was in the best company.

Z had begun the evening sitting just two rows in front of us. An hour after it had begun, he had apparently had enough because he walked out and never returned.

June fell asleep about halfway through.

Subi and I began the movie like we had done with all the others, sitting next to each other with our bucket of popcorn. After Z had walked out, within just a few minutes, she leaned into me. I was surprised that she seemed to be making the first move, but it was such a subtle lean that I wasn't quite sure if that was what she was doing. Was she actually trying to get closer to me, or was she just shifting in her seat because she had sat in the same position for too long?

I figured the best way to find out would be to lean into her as well, and I put my arm around her. She immediately dropped her head onto my shoulder and left it there for the rest of the very long movie. I relished every moment.

There was a moment when her head tipped down and I wondered for a moment if she had fallen asleep, but then I felt the tip of her finger tracing up and down my forearm. I watched her do this for a few minutes before I turned my hand palm-up and fanned out my fingers. She slipped her hand into mine and leaned closer into my chest.

When the movie was over, I glanced over at June. She was still sitting in the same position she had been for the last hour, slumped down in her seat with her head on the back of the chair and her eyes closed.

I didn't want to be the first to move. I could stay in this position all night and love every second of it. Apparently, Subi was thinking the same thing because we remained in our seats all the way through the credits and even a few minutes afterward.

We awakened June and walked out to my pickup. As we were leaving the parking lot, when I reached over to slip the truck into second gear, she placed her hand on top of mine and left it there all the way home.

We said goodnight to June, and I accompanied Subi back to her house. As soon as we were inside her living room, she wrapped her arms around my middle and buried her head into my chest for a few minutes. She pulled her head back but kept her arms secured around me.

I moved in a few inches with hopes of stealing my first kiss, but she didn't respond in kind. She didn't pull away, but she didn't move in any closer either. Instead, she remained just where she was with our noses only inches apart. She kept her eyes locked into mine, reading me.

She didn't have to use words. She had an amazing ability to say more with her eyes than she could with her lips, and she lacked the ability to hold anything back as her eyes talked to me. I knew she wanted to kiss me as much as I wanted to kiss her, but her hands were tied. She needed this, and yet, we weren't allowed to have it.

"You'll understand soon," she said.

"Why not now?"

"I can't. Not yet."

She buried her head into my chest again for a long time before saying, "Have a night, Miles. Make it a good one."

I released my arms from around her, pulled the clicker from my pocket, and within two seconds I was back in my own room.

As tired as I was, I knew I wasn't going to be able to fall asleep until my mind could settle down, so I sat on the balcony and wrapped myself in a blanket.

There was a flock of about two hundred sanderlings running around on the shore. These little birds always cracked me up. I knew this was the way they hunted for tiny bits of food as the waves came in, but it always looked like a funny little game of playing chicken with the waves—as if they were seeing who dared to get closest to the wave without actually getting swept up.

I remembered playing a similar game as a child. My sister and I would pretend the waves were lava, and we would see just how close we could get to the lava without allowing it to burn us dead. We would follow the water as it retreated toward the ocean and then run for our lives when it would chase us back to try to burn us. As the lava rolled in, we would wave our hands in the air and scream with panic. Of course, part of the fun would be to let the lava catch us periodically so we could make believe we were melting in it. Then we would snap back to life and start over.

I wasn't any different now that I was a young adult. I was consumed with the idea of trying to catch someone who was uncatchable. She made that much clear. She also made it clear that the more I tried to chase her down, the closer I tried to get, the more likely I was going to get burned.

Like the silly little sanderlings, it was all worth it just to find tiny bits of treats in the sand.

FIFTEEN

I spent a few minutes talking to Amos in the morning about which direction he would like me to go. I pulled up a map of the region and let him decide that his favorite drive would be straight down the coast into California. As the summer warmth would come upon us in a month or two, we could then build his world up north into Washington, or maybe even a few hundred miles up the coast of Canada.

"The Redwoods," he said as he sat on his balcony railing. "You would be doing me a huge favor if you were to expand Olinc all the way down and around the California Redwoods. I would be greatly in your debt."

"You won't be in my debt. Friends just do things for each other. If I know that you enjoy your ride, that's enough payback for me."

"Friends?" He scoffed. "We aren't friends. Maybe someday, but we're not friends. Not yet. You don't know me."

"We're friends."

"Are you going to ride in this weather?" he asked, holding one hand out as drops of rain began to hit him.

"I was planning to ride the Harley, but no. I don't feel like freezing in the rain today. We are friends, but my friendship has limits when it comes to the cold."

"We're not friends," he reiterated, but I could hear a tone of pleasantry in his voice.

"Be careful in this rain," I said. "If your balcony railing gets wet, you're going to slip right off there and ... *splat*!" I clapped my hands together like I had seen him do in the past.

He took a drag from his cigarette and flicked the ashes out in front of him. "If you ever find me splattered on the concrete below, you can rest assured someone pushed me."

"That's morbid."

"I'm being serious. I live up here between life and death, but I don't have a death wish. If you find me down there on the ground in a bloody heap," he pointed a finger at the ground below, "then that means someone pushed me."

"Who would push you?"

"Anyone who doesn't like me. Anyone who knows I could undo all this Olinc nonsense. Maybe Z. Maybe your girlfriend." He turned away from me and put his hand out again to feel the rain.

I didn't feel like continuing this conversation any further. I left Amos's room with a weird feeling in my stomach. What did he mean he could undo Olinc? I knew I didn't have the power to undo any of this, and he seemed like he had even less power than I had. What did he know that I didn't know?

He was obviously more observant than I thought he was. I never saw him outside his room, and I never saw him speaking to anyone else, so where was he getting the idea that Subi was my girlfriend? She wasn't actually my girlfriend, but he clearly knew there was something there, even if I didn't quite know what label to give it.

The cold rain pestered me as I took a few minutes to disconnect the motorcycle trailer from the back of my pickup truck. When I turned, I saw June wheeling herself down the walkway toward me. She looked like she had something to say, so I hurried over to meet her.

"What you're doing for Amos is a really beautiful thing," she said. "I want to help."

"Help? How can you help?"

"You're forgetting. I used to do your job before you took over." She pointed to the spot right behind her left ear. "Olinc reads my input too.

If you do the driving, and you focus on the road in front of you, and I watch out the passenger window, then we get twice as much data during the drive."

"And on the drive back, your passenger side window will be the other side of the road. You're right. That would be a really big help."

I helped her into the cab of my pickup, loaded her wheelchair into the back, and we set off together.

It was nice to have a partner along for the drive. As much as I was happy to help Amos by building his long stretch of scenic road, the concept never really appealed to me. Whether I was in my pickup, or on a motorcycle, or an airplane, or train, or whatever it might be, the idea of travelling was always rather boring to me. Even if I had the sound of the Harley-Davidson purring beneath me and the wind on my face with beautiful country all around me, travelling was just travelling to me. I didn't understand the appeal. So, having June here with me for the day was a really nice surprise.

The rain hammered us for most of the day, so we didn't bother making any scenic stops. We pulled up to quite a few gas stations and refilled the tank more often than we needed to just so Amos would have a lot of options to fill up along the way, but for the most part the day was spent just driving and driving and driving.

As we were coming up on Newport, which left us about half an hour away from home, I could sense that June had something on her mind. She would periodically look over at me, then turn back toward the window without saying anything. Sixty seconds later, she would do it again.

"Are you worried about something?" I asked. "You look like you're worried."

She turned toward me, her face devoid of the usual radiant smile. "Be careful around Amos. He can't be trusted."

"What do you know about him? He's a bit of a mystery to me. I can't quite figure him out."

She shook her head. "I don't think I know anything you don't know. In fact, I'm sure I know less than you do because you talk to him, and I just observe him from a distance. But I know they keep him around for a reason. I just don't know what that reason is."

"I think Z wants to fix him. Z has a funny obsession about fixing people."

"Amos doesn't want to be fixed, clearly."

"I think that's what Z likes about him. He likes the challenge."

She took a deep breath and turned to face her window. "Be careful around Z too. A lot of stuff happens around Z that ..." her voice trailed off.

"What kind of stuff?" I asked after waiting a long time in vain for her to finish that sentence.

"I've known Z since he was about ten years old. He is a sweet boy most of the time. All the time, actually." She turned back to face me again. "He's always sweet to everyone, but things just happen around him that I can't explain. People end up in jail. People end up hurt. People end up losing their businesses."

"That doesn't make him sound very sweet to me."

"It's never his fault. It's never him who does it. I can't explain it. He really is a sweet boy. Just—" She sighed. "Just be careful."

I hadn't realized just how badly I needed a break from Lincoln City until I began spending time in Northern California. When June and I had gone down together in my pickup, the fact that we were together made it feel like I had brought a piece of Lincoln City with me, so I didn't feel like I was outside of the bubble. On the first day that I took the Harley-Davidson down, though, I was like a dog that had been kenneled for months and the gate was finally opened.

Amos had said he was only interested in the ride. Feeling the bike beneath him. The freedom of the road. He had said nothing about taking long walks through the majestic forests, and I doubted he would spend much time on nature hikes, but I began to explore the walking trails because *I* wanted to do it for *me*. If Subi or Z were to ask, I would tell them it was all part of expanding the world for Amos, but Amos really had nothing to do with me wanting to explore.

The beauty of the Redwoods didn't even have much to do with me wanting to explore. It was all about the liberty of being far away from all the confusion and uncertainty.

Being on the bike and walking through the woods gave me ample opportunity to sort myself out through self-reflection. I appreciated that time. I still didn't care much for riding a motorcycle just for the sake of riding, but I was beginning to see why it appealed to others.

With so much time for pensiveness, I couldn't help but wonder where Amos's mind would go during such long rides. While my thoughts were mainly consumed with the idea of falling in love, I couldn't think of anything he cared deeply about except for tobacco. I thought about him so much that I resolved to figure out a way to pry into his mind after he went for his first long ride.

I ended up staying in California for two nights and rode home late on the third day. On top of wanting to have some time away, I also wanted to see what would happen if I pushed the boundaries of my freedom. I wanted to know what would happen if I left in the morning without telling anyone when I would be coming back, and then I just didn't come back. Nobody had ever told me I had a curfew. I wanted to test out Amos's hypothesis that I was still locked up in a jail cell—except that it happened to be a very large prison.

It wasn't until an hour after the sun had set for the night, and I was comfortable in a hotel room with a television remote in my hand, that my phone finally rang. Subi was calling to check on me. I had already known they would know exactly where I was. When they had given me my cell phone at the start of it all, they had told me that there was a tracker on it. They had probably tracked me and followed my movements numerous times before as I went around mapping out Olinc, but this was the first time anyone had ever called to check on me.

She didn't chastise me or lecture me in any way. Quite the contrary, actually. She praised me for going the extra mile with building Amos's world for him. Yet, although she didn't say anything about taking time for myself or needing some distance, I knew I wasn't fooling her. She would say things like, "Take as much time as you need to map out the Redwoods," and we both knew what she really meant.

On that second night, I heard a certain hint of longing in her voice when she called. Our conversation the previous evening had only lasted about five minutes, but our call that second night lasted for nearly two hours—far too long to be able to say she was just calling to "check on me." A handful of times our chat paused after exhausting a topic and we would find ourselves in silence for a long span, but neither of us wanted to say goodnight, and one of us would come up with something new to discuss.

When we had both finally grown tired, she said her familiar words, "Have a night," and I jumped in to finish the phrase, "and make it a good one."

I chose to ride home late in the evening on that third day. I had made that decision the night before. My reasoning was that I wanted a good amount of riding time in the dark because I hadn't yet spent any time collecting nighttime data on the Harley.

That decision made the day feel very long to me. I had already spent so much time walking the Redwoods that by lunchtime I didn't feel like taking that stroll any more. I had already checked out of my hotel room, so I didn't have anywhere to take a nap. From where I was starting, the ride would take me about six and a half hours to get back to Lincoln City.

My original plan was to try to make it home at about 11:00 at night to gather the data I wanted. That meant I would need to leave somewhere around 4:30, but after I finished my lunch, I just couldn't take it anymore. I decided to get started earlier, and then I would take extra time to stop at any and every sight along the way.

The feeling of needing the distance and time alone was gone now. I wanted my own bed. I wanted my balcony overseeing the seagulls and the sanderlings. I wanted my own familiar spot on the ocean back.

I missed Subi.

Unfortunately, I knew she usually went to bed pretty early. I thought that rolling in at 11:00 was probably too late to give me a chance to see her before calling it a night, but I was wrong. From a distance, long before I pulled the bike into the parking lot, I looked up to see her familiar shape in the dark. She was standing in the center of the parking lot with her cell phone in hand.

SIXTEEN

I rode the motorcycle up next to Subi. When I looked at the cell phone in her hand, I saw a map of Lincoln City on the screen. I knew she had been tracking my movements, waiting for me to make it back home.

She wrapped her arms around me even before I had finished taking off my helmet. "I know it's late, but I need you tonight," she said.

I hadn't been able to see it in the dark, but I could feel in her embrace that she had been crying. "Are you okay? Tell me what's going on."

"Go ahead and park the motorcycle." She followed me to the nearest parking spot.

I asked her if she wanted to go into her place, or if she would rather go up to mine. She took me by the hand and pulled me toward the stairs that led up to my room.

"Take a hot shower," she said, letting go of my hand once we were in my room. "You need it."

I was a bit surprised. Whatever was eating at her was urgent enough that she would wait for me in the center of the parking lot. "Are you sure? A shower can wait."

"I can feel it on your skin." She placed one hand to my cheek and held it there for a few seconds. "You're ice cold from your ride. It's enough for me to know you're here. I'm good."

I stripped myself of my leather outer layers, grabbed a change of clothes, and slipped into my bathroom.

She was right. A large percentage of my body was numb and had been for the last two hours. For half the ride home, I had been mumbling to myself that Amos had better appreciate what I was doing for him.

I winced in pain as the hot water stung my icy skin. On another day, I might have turned the heat down and ramped it up slowly as my body grew accustomed to it, but today I had Subi out there waiting for me. Anything I could do to speed up this thawing process was worth the discomfort of a thousand needles jabbing into me.

I emerged from the bathroom to find the lights in my room all turned off and Subi sitting out on the balcony. "These chairs are the worst," she said. "We need to get you some sort of weather-resistant loveseat."

"I'd like that." I pulled my chair up next to her and waited for her to spill whatever was brimming over in her mind.

"I'm failing at this." She leaned her head onto my shoulder. "I started working on Olinc years ago when I was just out of high school. Back when it was just Ramsey and me. I had specific goals in mind—especially one specific goal—and I just can't get there. Today was a major blow. I'm failing."

I was baffled. What could she possibly mean? From what I could see, she was building the most amazing system imaginable. The kind of thing I would never even be able to think up, let alone make it a reality.

"What on earth are you talking about? A week ago, I couldn't get a grumpy blind man to come out of his room. Then, after just a few days of working on my part—wait, scratch that. I shouldn't even call it work. All I had to do was take a road trip. After a few days of taking a road trip, this crotchety blind man is going to relive his dream of going across the country on a Harley-Davidson." I squeezed her hand. "You did that. Not me. Not Z. Not even your team. You did that."

She squeezed my hand back and said nothing. We watched a flock of sanderlings down below as they chased the waterline back toward the ocean and then scurried away every time a new wave rolled in toward them. "Run for your lives!" she said quietly in a high-pitched voice, allowing for a smile and a small laugh to temporarily cover up her frustration.

"Seriously," I said. "How could you possibly call yourself a failure?"

"Did you know that NASA invented all kinds of things when they were trying to get us to the moon for the first time?" she asked. "The more they tried to plan a trip to the moon, the more they ran into problems, and discovered new issues that would keep them from getting there. They had to invent a whole bunch of things all along the way. The technology that led to things like the digital camera, water purification systems, wireless technologies, and all kinds of stuff came from those missions. The main goal was to get to the moon, though." She let go of my hand and leaned forward to rest her elbows on her knees, shaking her head. "Olinc is a byproduct of what I've been trying to accomplish for years. Olinc is nice, but it's a water purification system. It's not the moon."

"Are you listening to yourself right now? If humanity had never been able to reach the moon, do you really think that would have meant it was a complete failure?"

"Well, yes."

"Water purification systems. Digital cameras. Satellites. Whatever inventions are on that list ... this world is so much better because of the things you're talking about." I placed one hand on her back. "We all use our cell phones every day, and probably a bunch of these other things from that list too. But it's pretty rare that I find myself thinking about how we went to the moon."

She turned to me, and I could see pain in her eyes. She leaned back and grabbed my hand again.

"Tell me what your moonshot is," I said. "If Olinc is a byproduct of whatever it is you're trying to achieve, what is it you're really shooting for?"

She took in a deep breath and held it there. I could see for a moment that she was trying to hold back the tears, but one came anyway. It slid down her left cheek just before she said, "To give my dad a few more years of joy before we would lose him."

That was quite the bombshell. She had never mentioned her father before, let alone the fact that he was apparently not long for this world.

A list of questions began to form in my mind, but I knew she would answer them at her own pace.

"I lost Mom when I was young. I have only a few memories of her. My dad is my hero. My best friend. He has always been my biggest cheerleader for everything." She grabbed my arm and placed it around her, nestling into me even though the uncomfortable armrests of our cheap chairs jabbed into our sides. "Midway through my senior year of high school, he went in for a checkup because he was having trouble with a few things. Ever since we got his diagnosis, my goal has been to figure out a way to give those with Parkinson's disease a new lease on life. I have invented all kinds of things along the way, but the moon feels even farther away now than it did when I began this journey."

"I don't know much about Parkinson's disease. Why is it June can walk around inside Olinc, but it doesn't work for your dad?"

"I admit I have to rely on the brain specialists for a lot of what I do—our team of surgeons you met in the operating room. A lot of what they say goes right over my head. But my understanding is that June's handicap is because of a problem in her spinal cord. There's nothing at all wrong with the way her brain functions. The implant we use with Olinc plugs into her brain."

"Same with Amos?"

"Same with Amos," she agreed. "But Parkinson's disease is a result of there being something wrong with the nerve endings inside important parts of the brain. Trying to give Dad an implant has been like trying to plug a regular extension cord into a badly misshapen wall outlet."

Something hit me at that moment. There was a reason this was boiling over today. "Did your dad take a turn for the worse today?"

She nodded without looking up. She reached a hand up and wiped at her eyes. "He is not expected to make it through the night. Two days at the most."

"Then you need to be back home. I can go with you if you want. We can leave right now. We'll take my truck." I shifted in my seat to get up.

She sat up straight but made no effort to stand. "Things are more complicated than that."

"Subi, I can't pretend to understand the complexities of your relationship, but don't let your father pass away without you there. You would regret that for the rest of your life. You said yourself that you two were inseparable."

"We still are. It's just ... you'll understand someday."

I didn't know what to say to that. When I arrived home less than an hour ago, I wanted nothing more than a hot shower and my pillow for the night. Now I was willing to forgo a night's sleep altogether to get her home to Idaho on what seemed to me like one of the turning points of her life, but she shot the idea down outright. It made no sense.

After ten minutes of long silence, she stood up and grabbed me by the hand to pull me to my feet. She stepped behind me as I pulled open the sliding glass door, and we both walked into my room. I began to walk toward the front door, but she pulled on my hand and walked me to my bed.

We lay down together on top of the covers. She kicked off her shoes and nestled into me. I felt a closeness with her in that moment that I had never been able to experience before, but my emotions were confusing and complicated. I wanted to let this moment be the catalyst for taking our relationship to the next level, but the thought of stealing my first kiss in the vulnerable moments surrounding her father's death made me feel like a selfish monster.

"I didn't know how much I needed you before," she said. "Thank you for being ... you."

We lay there in that same position for a long time. I could tell the moment she fell asleep because her hand loosened within mine. With her head nestled into the nook of my shoulder, I felt her breathing begin to deepen.

I remained perfectly still to not disturb her sleep. She needed this respite right now a lot more than I needed a comfortable position.

I remained alert for most of the night in my thoughts. I still wasn't sure what our relationship was. She had drawn solid lines she wouldn't let me cross, and yet, she needed me just as much as I needed her.

Tomorrow was going to be a big day. I was excited to see if I could finally nudge Amos into connecting himself to Olinc. Tomorrow was destined to be life-changing for him, and I looked forward to watching that happen.

On the other hand, tomorrow would likely be when Subi would get the news that the day she had been dreading was now here. Tomorrow was destined to be a life-changing day for her, and it pained me to think about that.

SEVENTEEN

We were awakened in the morning to the sound of someone knocking on my door. When I bolted upright in surprise, I felt a kink in my right shoulder as a result of sleeping in such an awkward position. I had only slept for perhaps three and a half hours or so, and I had awakened a handful of times during that period with my shoulder begging for a new position. Still, I didn't want to move her.

"Who is it?" Subi asked with her eyes half open.

"No idea." I took a second and sat at the end of my bed to gather my bearings before making my way to the door.

Amos stood there in my doorway, fully dressed out in his riding gear. "I heard you roll in last night on the hog. Are you finished with your riding? Is it ready for me to try it on the roads?"

"Yeah." I wiped at my eyes with the backs of both hands. "You know, you don't really have to wear all that leather right now. You won't be riding out here in the real world, so you only need to put it on once you're inside Olinc."

"But if I'm wearing all this when I plug in, I'm already dressed when I get in there. Isn't that how it works?" he asked.

"I suppose so." I couldn't help but grin at this. He was like a child on Christmas morning, standing at his parents' bedside, asking if it was time to go out to the living room to see if Santa had come.

I normally would have felt irritated by someone knocking on my door after what felt like ten minutes of sleep, but I was relieved and excited to see Amos brimming over with enthusiasm like this. Up until now, I had wondered if he would go through with it, or if I had been doing all that work for nothing.

"Get dressed. I will meet you up in my room in five." He felt for the railing and began walking toward the stairs.

I didn't have to change my clothes since I was still in my clothes from the night before, but there was no way of him seeing that. I turned back toward my room and saw Subi sitting there on the edge of my bed. Her hair was a bit disheveled, and her eyes still looked tired, but she never looked more gorgeous.

"How are you feeling?" I asked.

She rose to her feet and walked over to me. She turned her head to one side and buried her cheek into my chest with her arms around me. "Today is going to be a hard day. Dad is still with us, but not for long."

I wondered how she could know this so confidently and assumed she must have read a text message or two while I was chatting with Amos. "Do you want to come up to Amos's room with me? I think he's actually going to go through with this. I think he's really going to connect to Olinc."

"It does sound like a lot of fun, but no. I don't think I'll join you. Amos doesn't like me. He doesn't trust me." She pulled her head away from my chest enough to look me in the eye. "You've done a good job with him. He trusts you."

"Are you sure? Watching a blind man experience sight again after so many years of not being able to see ... it's going to be special."

She smiled. "It will be. I don't want my presence to screw that up. It's got to be just you." She pressed her cheek again to my chest and gave me a squeeze before turning back toward the bed. She slipped her shoes on, then made her way to the door. "I'll be at my place if you need anything. I'll be tracking him from my station."

When I turned around to put on my shoes, she slipped out so quietly that I didn't realize she was gone until I looked up again.

It felt strange to be the only one there with Amos on his big day, but Subi was obviously right. When I thought about what it would be like to have a room full of people eagerly awaiting his moment, I could easily picture him refusing to go along with any of it just because they wanted him to. We would be running the risk of him slamming the door on that possibility forever.

As I climbed the stairs to his room, I decided the best thing would be to focus all my words on the motorcycle and the ride he would be taking. I would talk as little about Olinc as possible, even if that meant avoiding talk about him receiving his sight again.

I found Amos's door already open when I arrived at the top of the stairs.

"It's a smooth ride," I said. "That bike purrs like a kitten."

"I hope that's not true. Harleys—they're supposed to growl like an angry dog." Amos let out a loud growl of his own.

I couldn't help but smile at this side of him. "Okay, then. It's like sitting on the back of a junkyard dog. Let's get you on that bike."

"So. All I need to do is stick this end of the wire to the spot here on my neck?" He connected the end of the wire behind his ear.

"And then press the button on your clicker." I grabbed his clicker from the nightstand and placed it in his hand.

"I can wait," he said. "You go connect yourself to the machine. Meet me back here in three minutes on the other side."

"Sounds good. I'll be right back. There's no need to be nervous," I said as I hurried toward the door.

"I'm not nervous," his voice said from behind me.

I sprinted to my room, lay on my bed, connected myself to Olinc, and was back up in his room as quickly as possible. I was sure I had successfully returned within the three-minute time limit he had given me, but he had obviously changed his mind about waiting. I found him already standing at the foot of his bed with his helmet under one arm.

He sized me up as I came into the room.

Having never seen my face before, I realized he may not be 100% sure it was me who stood in front of him, so I spoke just so he could hear my voice. "How are things? Can you see?"

"I see." He slowly looked around. He walked around looking at different things that I would normally not pay much attention to like the generic hotel art on his wall, texture in curtains, and the patterns of the floor tile.

He pulled open the curtain, and I was able to see his eyes grow wide at the sight of the ocean. He caught me smiling as I watched him, and he quickly pulled the curtain back closed.

"I'm ready." He placed his helmet on his head, fastened the strap snugly, and walked out the door. He grabbed hold of the railing as he walked, just like he would have if he didn't have his new eyes and took his time descending the stairs.

"She is gorgeous," Amos said just before reaching his last stair. He walked over to the bike and squatted down next to it. He felt it with his hands as he looked it over. "She looks just like the picture I had in my mind. She is beautiful."

"Fire her up. Let's hear her growl like a junkyard dog."

Amos took another second to finish checking out every inch of the bike before throwing one leg over the seat and straddling it. He gripped the handlebars, stood up, placed his right foot on the kick-start, and stomped the engine to life. It roared that familiar sound I had heard so many times over the last few days. He twisted the throttle with his right hand and the roar of the engine echoed through the parking lot.

For a split second, I worried it was too early in the morning to be making this type of noise before I remembered we were the only two people in this world.

"Yes! Yes!" I yelled.

Amos let off on the throttle and the engine quieted to a grumble. He pushed back with his feet and walked the bike backward about ten steps. He put two fingers to his eyebrow and gave me a playful salute before kicking into gear and lifting his feet as the bike rolled forward. He turned toward the entrance of the parking lot and took it easy for the first few seconds, but by the time he was halfway down the road, he was at full speed.

I stood in the center of the parking lot watching him grow smaller and quieter in the distance. Seeing him ride away on that bike felt like I had just crossed a finish line that not only had felt so far away but also felt like I had to search and search to even know where to find it. It had been an exhausting emotional experience just to get this far, and I couldn't shake the feeling that this marathon was far from finished.

Z had previously tried to explain why Amos's progression was so important to him, but I had never been able to connect with his reasoning. It was a noble and a beautiful thing to want to help a blind man see, and to help a felon reform into a better man, but Amos didn't want the help. Surely there were countless blind, or deaf, or handicapped people out there who would give anything to have this opportunity.

Amos was out there finally taking advantage of a small piece of what Olinc had to offer, but I had no faith that he was any closer to letting Z mold him into someone different than who he was.

I pulled the clicker from my pocket, pressed the button, and I was immediately back on my own bed in the real world.

I continued to lay on the bed for a few minutes just staring straight up at the ceiling. The exhaustion of getting such a short and irregular night's sleep was weighing heavily on me now, and I wanted to just stay in this position for the rest of the day to give myself some rest.

I couldn't shake Subi from my mind, though. Today was likely to be one of the turning points in her life, and I didn't want her to feel alone. There wasn't a whole lot I could do, but I had to at least check on her before I lay down to catch up on some sleep.

I rolled to one side and placed my feet on the floor. I grabbed a poppyseed muffin from atop my mini-fridge, and a pint of milk from inside of it, and began devouring my breakfast as I walked down the stairs. By the time I reached her front door, I had an empty muffin wrapper in one hand and only two inches of milk left in my bottle.

I knocked very softly. She hadn't slept a whole lot more than I had last night, so I didn't want to wake her if she was asleep in her bed.

It wasn't long, though, before I heard her muffled voice through the door telling me to "Come on in." I stepped through the doorway to find her standing a few steps inside the door.

"Thanks for checking in on me." Behind her bright signature smile there was pain in her eyes. "Dad is still with us. He's in and out of consciousness right now, but he's still with us."

"Is there anything I can do? Anything you need?"

"I need you. I just need you to be present. I don't think I can handle being alone today." She pinned both of her arms into her chest and leaned into me. "Is there anything you need to do, or anywhere you need to be today? I could come with you."

I wrapped both of my arms around her and gently squeezed. "I'm taking the day off to do whatever I want today. I'll be here if this is where you want me. Or if you need to go anywhere else ... whatever you need."

"Thank you for being ... you."

"I would like to keep a bit of an eye on Amos," I said. "You said there is a way for you to track his location, right?"

"Take a seat on the couch." Subi walked over to her workstation and began clacking away at her keyboard.

The television screen that hung on the front wall of her living room lit up with a map of Oregon's west coast. Along the black line that indicated Highway 101, there was a red dot with a picture of Amos's face next to it. It was moving slowly down the line with a small caption beneath it reading "55 mph."

"He's only going 55 miles per hour," I said. "He's not in much of a hurry to get anywhere."

"He's just riding for the sake of riding," Subi said from behind her monitors.

We watched the dot move ever so slowly for a few minutes before Subi stepped in front of me.

"I know you're exhausted," she said. "I can't tell you how much it means to me that you would come down here rather than catch up on sleep in your own bed." She pointed to a blanket folded up on the floor next to the couch. "This couch is nice and wide. It's great for naps.

Make yourself a little more comfortable. Catch up on some sleep if you want to. Or watch a movie. Whatever you need."

"What are you going to be doing?"

"Nothing motivates progress like being in crisis mode. Today I'm in perpetual crisis mode. Hopefully I'll be able to make some sort of breakthrough that will someday help me reach the moon."

I sat on the sofa and asked the TV for a list of documentaries it had on file. With Subi's father on my mind, I wasn't in the mood for any true crime murder shows or stories about dead celebrities. I settled on a series that highlighted the training of Navy SEALs. I caught no more than about ten minutes of it before I fell asleep.

After maybe an hour or so, I woke up to Subi sitting down next to me on the couch and then leaning in to nestle up to me. I pulled an arm out from under my blanket and wrapped it around her. She slid her hand into mine, interlocking our fingers.

"Dad isn't suffering anymore," she said softly. "Dad's gone."

EIGHTEEN

I gave Subi a gentle squeeze. I didn't know what it felt like to lose a parent, but that didn't mean I had never lost someone important to me. When I was eighteen, one of my closest friends died from a horrible accident in the Boise River. Just one day before, he and I had been laughing it up like we had always done since we were little, and then the next day I found myself trying, but failing, to accept the fact that we would never have that again.

I wanted to be strong for Subi at that moment. I wanted to be her rock, but so many memories flooded back into me in an instant that I couldn't help but mirror some level of her grief.

At one point, when I sniffled, she spun around in my arms to face me. I had no tears, but I was sure it wasn't hard to see the pain in my eyes.

"You want to know one thing Dad used to say to me all the time?" she asked. "Whenever we were having a discussion about boys, or when I was thinking about getting married, or whenever he was talking about his memories of Mom ... he would always say the same thing." She deepened her voice to mimic his and continued with, "Fall in love with someone who, when the worst day of your life comes, he is the one you need and want there with you."

"I'm here. Thanks for letting me be that for you today."

She tilted her head back so she could get a better look at me. Her expression of pain softened as she looked into my eyes.

Then came a knock at the door. Caught off guard, we both jumped a little. Subi asked me to answer it.

"Knock. Knock," came Z's voice from behind the door as I opened it. "Is everybody decent?" He wore a cheesy grin, but when he saw Subi lying on the couch with blankets and an empty spot next to her where I had obviously just been, his face snapped back in surprise. He looked at me a bit differently than he ever had before, then at Subi, and back at me again.

"Good morning, Z," Subi said.

"I—" he looked back and forth between the two of us a few more times before his expression changed back to normal. "I was just looking for you, Miles. I thought I would find you here. I wanted to congratulate you on such a job well done with Amos. Astounding. Absolutely astounding. I don't think any of the rest of us would have been able to pull off what you have done. Definitely not in such a short period of time, if at all."

"I'm glad I was able to contribute," I said. "I don't know what difference it will make, but I'm glad I was able to help out a little."

"You don't know what difference it will make?" Z scoffed. "There is a blind man out there on a Harley-Davidson cruising down the Pacific coast toward the redwood forests of California. That's life-changing stuff right there."

"True," I said, "but I don't know how life-changing it will be. I have a feeling he's still going to be good ol' crotchety Amos who hates everybody and trusts nobody, even after he has been riding for years."

"I don't think I have ever seen him smile, but I can picture in my mind what it probably looks like," Z said. "That's enough for me right now. That's all I need."

"I can picture it too," Subi added. "If he's smiling, his teeth are probably filled with bugs. This is Oregon in May, after all."

We all shared a laugh at that.

"Sue, can I steal you for a moment?" Z asked and nodded his head toward the back of the house.

I felt weird being the only one left in her living room while they were back in the hallway talking. It should have been me who stepped outside to leave the two of them to have a word.

"What do you think you're doing?" I could clearly hear Z say from down the hall.

There was a long pause before Subi answered, "My father passed away today. I need ... I can't be alone today."

"I'm sorry for your loss, but really. How do you think this is going to turn out?" Z asked.

"The experiment is over," Subi said. "Everything we have needed to test has been done. We have monitored Miles's reactions to everything, and everything has been working perfectly."

"Everything is not done. You know that," Z said.

"I'm sorry," Subi said, "but I don't share in whatever experiment you have going on with Amos. He clearly doesn't want to be part of this anyway."

"I know you don't. But it matters to me," Z said. "Besides, if you actually care about Miles, you won't do this to him. You won't let him fall for you when he can't have you. Think about that."

There was a short span of silence before Z and Subi were back in the room. He walked past me toward the front door and then just stood there as if he were sizing me up for the first time. The awkwardness of this stare got to me after a few seconds, and I turned away to look at Subi. By the time I turned back around, I was glad to find he had slipped out.

"How much of that did you hear?" she asked.

I said nothing in response, which told her all she needed to know.

"It's true. The things he said are true," she said.

"That I can't have you?"

She nodded.

"Because of your ex-husband?"

"No." She hurried to my side and grabbed my left hand with both of hers. "It's nothing like that. My ex-husband is long since out of this picture. There is no other guy."

"Then what? He said that if you actually care about me, you wouldn't let me fall for you. It's definitely too late for that. You are already part of me, so why are you saying I can't have you?"

"Someday you are going to go back to Idaho, and I will not."

"When am I going back to Idaho?"

"You're free to go back whenever you want. You could go back today if you so choose."

I shook my head. "This is where I want to be. Problem solved. I have no reason to go back to Idaho."

"You will. You'll want to go back." She rubbed the back of my hand with her thumb and turned her eyes away.

"None of this makes any sense. What am I missing?"

She shook her head. "I guess there are still a few things Z wants to know before we can fill you in on all the details. If you ask me, the experiment has run its course, but not if you ask him. Even I don't know what he's waiting to see. You'll know soon enough, and then you'll be ready to go back home."

I would be lying if I said our conversation didn't change the feeling between us. Within a few minutes, I was again alone on her sofa, and she was back at her working desk. The television in front of me was showing military men jogging in formation along the beach, but my mind was far away from whatever was on the screen.

When my mind reverted back to the reason I was spending the day with her, I reminded myself that she needed loving company today. She had just lost her father. Even if I knew for certain that I couldn't have her forever, I wanted to still give her my presence today.

I didn't know what my future held, though. From the best I could put these pieces together, it seemed like she was saying she wanted to be with me, but she didn't believe I would want to be with her anymore after this experiment was all finished. I couldn't fathom what revelation they could possibly give me that would drive me to want to leave Subi behind and head back to Idaho where nobody was waiting for me. She was everything I had ever wanted in a girl. She was always pleasant. Always fun. Brilliant. Drop-dead gorgeous. And above all, she had my full confidence and trust. There was no way I could believe this girl would have led me into an experiment that would leave me wanting to run away from her at the end. No way.

We spent the entire day together in her living room. She was back and forth between her workstation and sitting on the couch with me as we binge-watched season one of an old series called *24* that had been released in the early 2000s. I called for a pizza to be delivered around lunch time, but she didn't have any appetite, so I was the only one who ate from it. When dinnertime came, she made herself a light salad and I continued working on the Meat Lover's pizza that had assumed room temperature by that time.

We periodically checked in on Amos throughout the day by seeing where his dot appeared on the map. When he had left in the morning, I expected to see him return around nightfall, but that wasn't how things unfolded. As sundown came and went, we could see he was cruising the side roads around the redwood forests. It wasn't until past 9:00 that my cell phone chimed to let me know Amos had sent me a text.

"I'm glad he knows he has the ability to do that," Subi said.

His text message simply asked me what hotel I had stayed at. I responded by telling him where I had stayed and what room number, and then I asked him how his ride was going.

He gave no response to my question, but we saw his dot move all along the map until he was at the correct hotel. His dot didn't move any more that night.

"Thanks for being here for me today," Subi said as we stood in her doorway. "Have a night. Make it a good one."

We took a few steps toward the parking lot before she pointed at her door and asked me to shut it.

"You're very welcome." I held out my arms, and she quickly nestled into my chest again. I hadn't planned to hold her there for very long, but I sensed no urgency from her about me letting go. Since I was in no rush, we just stood there together for a long time.

I leaned my head back but didn't let go. She did the same, and our noses were only inches apart. I leaned in to finally steal that kiss she had been keeping from me, but she tipped her head forward so that my lips gently met her forehead instead.

"I'm sorry," she said. "I want to, but ... I've already pulled you into this so much further than I should have. You're going to go up to your room, and you're going to think about that conversation I had earlier with Z, and then tomorrow you'll want nothing to do with me."

"I would be lying if I said I wasn't nervous about whatever secrets you are keeping from me but tomorrow is tomorrow. I just spent the whole day thinking about your father and thinking about the times I had with someone I once lost. All I have of my old friend are memories from days past. I just spent the whole day wishing I could somehow have a chance to have one more day with him to build a new one." I pulled away from her enough to look her in the eye again. "Right now, I'm here with you. Sometimes we need to stop being scared of things that can hurt us and just take advantage of the moment."

I closed my eyes and leaned in halfway again so she could meet me there if she chose to. I felt her lean back at first, and for a brief moment I thought she was pulling away, but then I felt her hand on the back of my neck as her lips pressed into mine.

"I'm playing with fire. I know," I said once we separated. "You're worth it."

"I hope so." She leaned in again and stole a short second kiss from me before burying her head into my chest again. "Thank you for being ... you. Today has been one of the worst days of my life. I needed you today."

"I'll be here tomorrow." I took a step back from her porch.

I was quite a few steps away from her porch when I heard her say to herself so quietly that I didn't think she intended for me to hear, "I sure hope so."

All night, my head swam through the many thoughts inside of it. There was no way to calm the waters, but she had kissed me back. That, alone, was enough to keep me from drowning in my uncertainty.

The next morning, after a shower and another poppyseed muffin, I peeked out my door to see if the lights were on in Subi's house. Since they were, I hurried down the stairs and knocked on her door.

"Door's unlocked," she yelled from inside, and I let myself in.

I entered the house to see her standing in the center of the living room with her hands on her hips.

"How'd you sleep?" I asked.

"It wasn't the best sleep I've ever had, but I slept better than I thought I would." She pointed a finger at the TV on the wall. "I think we've got a problem."

I looked up to see Amos's dot again on the map. "He's on his bike. Going 64 mph. What's the problem?"

"Amos left first thing in the morning yesterday. He rode all the way down to the Redwoods and spent the day taking in all the backroads you had given him. This morning, he must have gotten up early and rode back toward home."

"Okay. So ... what's the problem?"

"Amos is going to starve himself to death. We have seen him stop a few times to get meals, but those meals are only Olinc meals. He could eat an entire elephant in there and it would do nothing for his natural body out here in the real world. Inside there, the program is set to taste the food, and even to feel like he's getting full, but out here in the real world nothing is changing."

"He's gone a full day without food. That won't kill him."

"But I sent him a text last night about it, and two more again this morning. No response. He's ignoring his phone on purpose. And now, look which direction his dot is moving."

Amos was about two hours north of the Redwoods, and now his dot was moving southbound again—away from home.

"Stubborn old man," I said. "He's going to starve himself to death."

"I don't know how long to let him go in there. I may need to disconnect him for his own good."

"That wouldn't go over very well. Is there a way for you to reset my drop spot? If I connect myself to Olinc, maybe instead of starting in my own room, I could pop in wherever he is. Then I'll have a little chat with him. That way he doesn't feel like anybody is jerking him around."

"Brilliant. That's a pretty simple adjustment. He had already stopped at a gas station for thirty minutes. I assumed that was to grab some breakfast. We'll just wait for him to stop somewhere for lunch and then hurry to get you there before he's back on the road again."

NINETEEN

It was hard to know when or where Amos would stop to eat. My previous assumption had been that he would ride down to the Redwoods, cruise some backroads through the forests, and then come back on the same day. Because of this, I hadn't spent a lot of time strategizing places for him to stop for food.

At a little after 1:00 in the afternoon, his dot stopped moving on the map.

"Hurry up to your room," Subi said. "Get ready, but don't get yourself linked in quite yet. It'll take me two or three minutes to reset your drop spot."

I hurried upstairs to my room and lay on my bed with the connection wire in one hand, and my cell phone in the other. As soon as her text message came through, I shoved my phone into my pocket, snapped the Olinc wire to the back of my head, and pressed the button on my clicker.

The ceiling of my room disappeared and was replaced by the overhead canopy of the most majestic trees in the world.

I sat up. This place was familiar to me since I had ridden up and down this road multiple times just two days ago.

At first, I worried that Amos had already ridden away, and we would have to try to catch him again later, but then I saw the back end of his Harley from behind a tree about a hundred yards away. I hurried toward him in case he was only stopping for a short time and was about to leave again.

He stepped out from behind the tree at the sound of my approaching footsteps. He had a large sandwich in his hand that was still halfway covered in the plastic wrapper.

"What are you doing here, boy? How did you even find me?" he asked.

"Everyone inside Olinc is tracked. It's built into the system."

"That figures."

"We have been trying to reach you. We sent you a few texts."

"I didn't want to be reached. I turned my phone off on purpose."

"So, have you been happy with how this works? With how this has turned out? I tried to get lots of backroads mapped out for you."

Amos seemed to be contemplating whether taking the effort to pay me a compliment was worth it. "Yeah. This is all good. Really good."

"Does it feel as good as you hoped it would?"

Amos's expression softened. "Boy, I gave up a long time ago on the hopes of ever having this again. Ever since I sold my old ride, I have had a recurring dream about being able to ride again. Sometimes I would have my old bike, sometimes a new one, but it was always the same thing. I would go to ride it, and something would be wrong. I would dream that the wheels were missing, or it was out of gas, or I couldn't get it kick-started no matter what I tried. Something along those lines for many years."

It amazed me that he spent so much time thinking and talking about this bike and never bothered to mention his eyesight. In my opinion, the view in Lincoln City along the oceanfront is one of the most beautiful sights in all the world. Standing at the foot of these redwoods had the ability to change a person's entire perspective—to make a person feel small and insignificant.

That all seemed to be lost on Amos. The world around him didn't seem to matter because he had his worldly possession. I had expected him to be a bit more like June. When she first got her legs back, someone could have put all the diamonds and fancy cars at her fingertips, and she would have ignored them all as she skipped like a schoolgirl down the sidewalk. I wondered if that would someday change for Amos as the novelty wore off.

"You have done well." Amos took another bite of his sandwich. "Do you plan to do more?"

"Sure. That's the plan. In time, I plan to add a lot more geography and detail all over the country."

He shook his head. "I am not talking about geography." He looked around as if he were checking to make sure nobody was hiding behind one of the trees. "You say they are tracking us, right?"

"Yeah."

"Are they listening in on us too?" He asked in a whisper. "Are they hearing every word we are saying right now?"

"No. I don't think so. There are lots of things I don't know about Olinc, but I've never seen anything that suggests they can hear what we are saying."

He thought for a second before continuing. "This world is great, but it could be a lot better."

"How so? Just tell me what kinds of pathways are your favorites. I bet we could get a few different motorcycles too."

"I'm not talking about pathways. The roads are great. The hog is great. I'm talking about this nice preschool you guys have built. It's designed for kids. It's made for people who are scared to have some real fun."

"I don't follow." I was confused, and yet I was pretty sure this conversation was taking a turn into somewhere I didn't want to go.

"This Olinc world. It is designed to see the earth, but it's not designed to experience the world." He looked all around at the forest surrounding him and smirked like it was nothing special. "Do you catch what I'm saying?"

I was beginning to understand, but I said nothing in response.

He held up his sandwich. "Look. When I am here inside Olinc, I can eat a sandwich, and it tastes exactly like I would expect an Italian sub to taste. I can taste every bit of the detail, right down to the spicy brown mustard. If this system has the ability to feed our taste buds and appetites, then why has nobody taken the time to really indulge in the true experiences of life? The only foods and substances that can be found inside Olinc are the ones you, June, and I have experienced. And yet, I am the only one who is willing to do any of the work to collect the good data. The only reason Olinc knows the taste of a cigarette is because of me." He patted his hand against his chest as he spoke. "You and June are like little kids. You don't go anywhere fun. I stopped at a few of the fine marijuana dispensaries along the way and I couldn't go inside because there wasn't any data inside the stores. Those places should be obvious stops for a world like Olinc."

"Smoking pot isn't my thing."

"Well, you're not doing a very good job with Olinc, then. This place needs the real experiences of life. It doesn't need a thousand destinations for sightseeing. What a waste. Live a little. Have some fun." He wrapped up his sandwich and set it on the back seat of his bike. He raised up a can of Heineken and patted his pocket where he kept his cigarettes. "I am glad to be able to get all the smokes and beer I want, but there is a lot more fun out there to be had. It is like living in a preschool in here."

I had never had a conversation about this sort of thing with Subi or Z. I didn't know how far Z would want me to take things in order to keep Amos happy in the Olinc system. The only thing I knew for sure was that if Amos were to be in charge of Olinc, then he would be requesting a long list of things I wasn't interested in trying. I was sure marijuana would only be a starting point.

"Smoking pot is just not my thing," I repeated.

"You don't need to smoke it. I have a mapping chip too, remember?" He pointed to the spot right behind his ear. "You just need to bring me stuff, and I'll do it."

"I keep forgetting about that. I've never asked Subi or Z what type of stuff they would allow."

"The only stuff they've let me have is cigarettes, pot, CBD oil, and a few select beverages. None of the really good stuff, for some reason.

That's it. I'm glad they let me have those, but those are just a teaser. They can only do so much for me."

"CBD oil and pot?" I wondered.

"This is Oregon and California we are talking about here. There is a marijuana dispensary on every block all the way down the coast, but you haven't been inside any of them. I need you to start visiting—" He stopped himself and waved away his comment with his hand. "Wait. I mean, Olinc needs you to visit all the good stores. As many as possible. That's a good place to start."

"Start? Where does it go from there?"

"Then we will go looking for some real fun. The stuff you can't get in the stores," he said with a smile. "Don't worry. Nobody is going to make you use it. If we can find some of what I want, then I will do the work of smoking it, or eating it, or injecting it."

"Injecting it?" Now we were talking about a whole new subject. If we were just talking about CBD oil or marijuana, and if Z and Subi were good with the idea of people using them inside Olinc, then I wouldn't have had a problem incorporating that into the data. But pot was not something people injected. What direction was he wanting to go with this?

"Yes. Injecting it," he said. "Stop being such a child. You were the one who asked me what my freedom would be."

"That isn't really what I meant."

"Then you have not thought about it enough." He closed his eyes and lifted his chin as if he were thinking about something far away. "When I was a younger man, I used to be able to ride with my boys across the country. We knew all the good places to stop. We knew where we could get anything we wanted. Nothing compares to the feeling of being doped up enough that we could ride for three days straight without needing to sleep. It's invigorating. It's the greatest rush this life has to offer. That is real freedom right there."

"It'll kill you."

He opened his eyes, looked at me, and pounded his fist into his hand. "And that is exactly what I am talking about! I lost a brother that way.

He was someone I rode with on every trip." He folded his arms across his chest and paused. "Then one day he overdid it. His heart stopped right there on the barroom floor. I can still see the scene clearly in my mind—his mama was slapping him in the face, telling him to wake up, while I was doing my best to perform CPR."

"That's terrible. I can't even imagine."

"But it doesn't have to be that way!" He balled up his fists and clenched his teeth. "I lost one of my brothers because we were doing that out there. There were risks to living the good life. But there are no risks inside Olinc. I thought we were free back in those days. I can only imagine how amazing it would have been to be able to truly live without having to worry about taking things too far."

"I—" I didn't know what to say. These were all things I had never thought about before, and I wasn't the least bit interested in participating.

"And that is just the start," he said. "Right now, there are very few people who have access to Olinc. Over time, once people see that they can live life to the fullest, a lot of people will be excited to be part of it. Imagine how great it would be if we could ride across the country, going for days without sleep, and having as many girls as possible all along the route. We wouldn't have to worry about STDs. There would be no unwanted pregnancies. We would not even have to worry about cops getting in the way of a good time." He pointed a finger at me. "It just all depends on whether you are willing to put in the work to build it. I can't do it on my own."

Again, I marveled at how he had a fresh new set of eyes, and yet he continued to look right past the best parts of his surroundings. I felt like I could spend every minute of every day building what I thought was the best experience, but none of it would appease him because he lived in an entirely different world from me.

"When we get back, we need to have a sit-down with Z and Subi to see what direction they want us to go," I said.

My comment clearly frustrated him, and I knew exactly what he wanted to say in response, but he bit his tongue.

"Look here. You have done a remarkable job. You are a hard worker, and you have a good eye for detailing this world. I appreciate you." He retrieved a pack of cigarettes from his breast pocket, pulled one out, and placed it in his lips. "Z and your girlfriend are in charge for now, but not forever. This world is too big and too powerful to contain."

This conversation had already been uncomfortable enough for me as it was. Now I was really worried about where it might be going.

"I have already been in contact with some other people about it," he continued. He cupped both hands around his cigarette as he put a small flame to the tip. "These other people ... they know how to have fun. They have plans to take it over and make it better. Much better."

"If they know how to do those kinds of things, then why don't they just build their own system?"

"They know things, but nobody knows how Olinc works. Not really." The tip of his cigarette glowed orange as he took a drag from it before putting the lighter back into his pocket. "Even Z doesn't know what makes the system work. Only your girlfriend knows that."

"How do you know this? I thought you were keeping yourself disconnected from all this Olinc stuff. I didn't think you were even interested."

"Olinc is great. I've always known that. I have mostly stayed out of it because I don't trust Z or Subi."

"You don't trust Z and Subi, but you trust a bunch of people who want to turn Olinc into one big rave?"

"If I am one of those in charge, yeah." He laughed. "And if I can get these other people what they need, then they say they will put me in charge of a lot of it. There is a lot of money to be made in all of this. There is a lot of fun to be had, too."

"What is it they say they need from you? What is it you can give them that they don't have? You want to let them dissect your brain to take a peek at your implant or something?"

He shook his head and blew a long puff of smoke above his head. "It's quite simple, actually. They have given me a hard drive. Their instructions are for me to reboot the Olinc system while the hard drive is plugged in.

While the system is booting up, the hard drive will record everything it needs to know. The whole ordeal should take only a few minutes. Then I would just give the hard drive to my guy, and they will do all the hard work from there."

"You really think it's that simple? You said yourself that Z doesn't know how it works. If all anyone needs to do is to plug in a hard drive and let it read the data while it boots up, then why hasn't anyone done it before?"

"The system is connected to the people who are part of the system. Some random person off the street could never use the main computer. If they were to touch it, nothing would happen. You, or me, or Z, or Subi—we all have a chip. The system knows its people."

I realized in that instant how stiffly I was standing. My feet were close together with my arms folded in front of my chest. It was at that moment that I decided to alter my approach. My mind had been darting from one idea to another, trying to figure out ways to talk him out of doing this, but I was sure there was nothing I could say to change his mind. A better tactic would be to make him think he was winning me over with this plan, and then to take my information to Z and Subi. I would let them decide what they wanted to do with all of this.

"Why are you telling me this?" I asked. "Seems like you could do this on your own and you wouldn't have to take the risk of telling me."

"Eyes." He flicked some ashes off the end of his cigarette. "I need your eyes."

"To shut the system down, you need to be able to read a computer monitor or something," I said, more of a statement than a question.

He nodded.

"And that's it? I shut it all down, plug in, reboot, and get out of there before anyone is the wiser?" I asked.

"That's it. Simple."

I didn't want to say outright that he could count me in. He was too smart for that. He would be suspicious if I said anything other than, "I'll think about it," which I did, and then after I was confident the conversation had come to its conclusion, I changed the subject to the initial reason I had popped in.

He wasn't as worried as I thought he would be about the idea of depleting his natural body out there in the real world. In fact, nothing I was saying was a surprise to him. His only response was that going a couple of days without food wouldn't kill him, and he would just get some good food once he got back, which he was planning to do by the end of today. Here inside Olinc he felt like he had a full belly, so he saw no issue with anything.

When I felt our conversation had reached its natural end, I said goodbye, pulled the clicker from my pocket, pressed the button, and was instantly back in my room.

Removing myself from that conversation and into the comforts of my own space felt like coming inside after having to walk home in wet and windy weather. I still felt drenched from the awkwardness of his proposal, but at least I could dry off for the time being.

Knowing that he was planning to be home somewhere around bedtime gave me plenty of time to sit down with Subi and Z.

TWENTY

Subi and Z both looked surprised that I called them together for a meeting at the conference table. I had never done that before. At first, they both looked a bit worried about what I might tell them, but as soon as I began filling them in on the details of the conversation I'd had with Amos, their expressions softened.

"You don't seem too worried," I said, looking back and forth between the two of them.

Subi shook her head. "Nah. It doesn't really work that way. They aren't going to learn anything at all from what you're describing."

"Then why does Amos think it's going to work?" I asked.

"Amos thinks he knows more than he does," Z said. "People have been trying to hack Olinc ever since its inception. Tons of people out there are trying to get inside it, but they can't. Not without an implant."

"Because the system knows its people," I said, repeating what I had heard Amos say.

Z nodded in agreement. "I'm more curious about who his contacts are. That would be nice to know so we can keep an eye on them. You have to keep your friends close, and your enemies closer."

"Oh, good heavens!" Subi cried, throwing her hands up in the air. "You're quoting The Godfather again?"

Z laughed. "How do you even know that's a quote from The Godfather? You've never even seen that movie."

"Everyone knows that quote. I don't even need to see the movie since you've practically quoted half of it to me over the years." She rolled her eyes.

"I'm just sayin'," Z continued with a laugh. "It would be nice to know who is trying to break into our system. And, you know, maybe head it off."

"Yeah. Okay," Subi said. "I think you're right. I'll put Tim on it."

I knew who Tim was. I sat next to him during most of the team meetings, but Subi and Z seemed to have some sort of automatic understanding of what needed to be done. It was as if they'd had this conversation before.

"I missed something," I said. "You guys seem to have this all planned out, but I have no idea what's going on."

"Whoever these people are," Subi said, "they think the information from a reboot will put them on track to creating their own Olinc. Or maybe they think they'll be able to hijack and take over our system. Either way, we should give them what they want."

"Well," Z added in, "we should give them what we *want* them to have. We make them think they're getting what they want. We will fill the hard drive with things that seem legit, but really it's just going to lead them down bad pathways that never get them anywhere near their goal."

"And in the process," Subi said, "when they open up and download all of the data, they will unknowingly be opening up their entire system for us to look inside it. We will be able to see anything we want to see."

"And we will be able to know who they are and where they are," Z said.

"So ..." I paused for a moment as I thought. "You want me to go ahead with whatever plan Amos has for me."

I was obviously a lot more nervous about this than Subi and Z. On top of the fact that I was still worried there might be something these two didn't understand, and that this plan might backfire into handing Olinc over to some sketchy people, I was worried what the repercussions might be of joining forces with Amos. I felt like I was strapping on a recording device to go undercover into some secret hideout of the

Cosa Nostra to gather some incriminating information. I didn't consider myself a very convincing actor. I was scared it would only be a matter of time before someone figured me out. I didn't even know who these people were, let alone what they would do to me if they discovered my allegiance was all a farce.

After our discussion, Subi disappeared into her house for a little while to talk to Tim and get things arranged for the download.

I sat up on my balcony and tried to let the waves calm me down like they had done so many times before, but I found myself restlessly getting up and pacing my floor until Subi finally knocked. With her there in the chair next to me, the waves were finally able to wash away some of my worry.

After a moment of long silence, as we sat there holding hands, out of the blue she began telling me a story of her father. It was a story of a long drive they had once taken to attend one of his high school reunions down in Arizona. I didn't have to listen very long to realize there was no big moral to this story, nor was there any punchline or surprise ending. It was just a random memory among what must have been a perpetual flood of memories flowing through her thoughts today.

With all that had been going on with Amos, I felt guilty that I had somewhat forgotten how close to the surface her heart must still be since it was only yesterday morning that her father had passed away.

I sat quietly for most of the evening, allowing her to skip from one remembrance to the next without interrupting her. He sounded like an amazing man. It was obvious that Subi had gotten her kind nature and pure heart from him. Above all, it was perfectly clear how much she loved him.

I repeatedly asked myself why she didn't want to be there at his side during his final moments. At one point I brought up the possibility of there being a memorial service to honor his life, but she brushed past the idea in a way that made it clear she wasn't planning to attend that either.

At a few minutes before midnight, she glanced at the clock and said, "I expect Amos will be home within twenty minutes or so. He doesn't trust me, so I'm going to head out just in case he comes here to talk to you. Make sure to stall him. Tim is going to work all night on getting things arranged for the download. Things should be good to go by sunrise."

"How will I know whether or not they're ready?" I asked.

"They'll be ready. Probably long before morning comes but hold off until sunrise just in case," she said. "If anything goes wrong with the preparations, I'll make sure you know."

I walked her to the door and pulled it open. She stepped outside and took two steps before spinning on her heel and hurrying back to me. She kissed me softly on the lips. It was short, but it said everything I needed to know, and then she hurried down the stairs.

I plugged myself into the Olinc system and waited for the sound of his Harley-Davidson to fill the air. Although time seemed to be moving a lot slower, I looked at the clock when he finally arrived and saw that exactly twenty minutes had passed since Subi left.

I expected it would only take a few minutes for Amos to come to my door, so I pressed the button on my clicker and found myself back in the real world, staring up at the ceiling from my bed.

As I waited for him to knock, I rehearsed in my mind some of the excuses I would give to keep Amos at bay until morning, but he never came. I had to wonder if he had clicked himself out of Olinc only to realize just how famished his body felt once he was back in the real world.

Once I no longer believed he would be coming to visit, I was able to slip under my covers and think myself to sleep.

I awakened in the morning to the sound of a seagull squawking as it perched on my balcony railing. I went through my morning routine of shower and breakfast, then decided I was done waiting for him.

I climbed the stairs to his room, knocked, and waited for him to answer. I heard him yell through the door that it was unlocked, and I stepped inside.

"Glad you made it home okay," I said as I walked through his room.

He was sitting on the edge of his railing again. I had been wondering if he would still do that after spending a few days on his motorcycle. Apparently, being out there living his best life was not enough to keep him from needing to walk the line between life and death. Or maybe perching himself there was just a matter of habit now.

"The ride home was just as good as the ride going down," he said.

"Being on the road that long didn't get monotonous to you? It doesn't get old?"

He ignored my question as he smashed his cigarette into the railing and then spun around to face me. He wasn't wearing his usual sunglasses, so his gray eyes pierced through mine even though he wasn't staring straight at me. "So, what did you decide about my proposal?" he asked. "Are you in?"

I didn't want to seem over-eager. "You swear by these people? I've never met them. I don't want to get in over my head."

"I swear by them, yes. Unless you are planning to take over. The only reason you would need to fear them is if you plan to double cross them. Are you the kind of guy who would try to take over?"

"Quite the opposite, actually. I'm no businessman. I don't want to run anything. I just want my cut of the pie and then I'm out. I'll be happy to take a few dollars and step aside for others to do whatever it is they want to do."

"Yes. In and out. Simple." He dropped down from the railing and stepped back into his room. He pointed to the nightstand next to his bed. "Open the drawer."

I opened the top drawer and pulled out an object about the size of a brick with a three-foot cable attached to it. "This is the hard drive?" I asked.

"That, it is."

"I don't know where to go. I don't even know where the main server is."

"Go down to the main lobby. Go to the same room where you have had all your team meetings. Go to the big front desk area where they used to check people in to the hotel."

"I know it. Yeah."

"Behind the front desk there is another room that is about ten feet by ten feet square. Everything you need is in there."

"Is there a whole bunch of other stuff in there too? Will it be obvious what I need to do?"

"There is nothing else in there. Shut the whole system down, not just the main computer. Shut down everything," he said. "After everything is shut down, plug in the hard drive. Then turn everything back on. There is a little light on the front of the drive that will be blinking while it is reading data. If it is still blinking, do not unplug it yet. When it is done blinking, go ahead and unplug. Then get out of there."

"What if someone catches me?"

"The people who run this place are geniuses, but they are simple. They are very trusting, especially toward you. If by chance someone catches you, just tell them you were curious about what was behind that door, and you accidentally shut the power down. Rebooting the system is not going to do any harm, so I seriously doubt anyone will think twice about it."

This was it. Hopefully Subi and Z knew what they were nudging me into.

I found my way to the room behind the front desk without any problem, and inside there was a large computer system just like I expected there to be. On the wall next to the computer tower was a black lever labeled "SYSTEM POWER."

I sat down at the desk and hit the spacebar on the keyboard to wake up the computer's monitor. The screen had all kinds of icons and information that meant nothing to me. I hovered over one icon at the bottom of the screen that looked like it might have something to do with rebooting the system, and a small menu popped up to give me the option of turning off or rebooting the system.

I knew I would need a moment after shutting things down to plug in the drive before turning it back on, so I opted to shut it down rather than just restart everything.

Upon making my selection, another warning appeared asking me again if I was sure I wanted to shut everything down, along with another line that read, "AFTER SELECTING POWER-DOWN MODE, HIT POWER BUTTON FOR COMPLETE SHUTDOWN."

I clicked on my selection again, watched my screen go blank, and then I pulled the SYSTEM POWER lever on the wall.

To my unpleasant surprise, everything went completely black. Not just the computer, and not just the system network.

Every light in the building shut off, and since I was enclosed in a ten-by-ten room with no windows, I couldn't see even the slightest outline of anything around me.

I began fumbling around for the hard drive. Upon finding it on the desk close by, I realized that I hadn't yet located the spot where I could connect the three-foot cable before turning everything back on. I grabbed my cell phone from my pocket and switched it to flashlight mode.

I kicked myself for not figuring this out beforehand. There were all kinds of little ports on the tower as well as on the desk itself where things could be plugged in. I began to feel a bit of panic but then reminded myself that the people in charge here were asking me to do this. If anyone were to discover what I was up to, it wasn't like I was going to be in trouble.

I tried all the ports one-by-one before stumbling upon one that fit the same size connector on the portable hard drive. I pushed it in and flipped the lever on the wall.

The lights on the ceiling came back to life, but the computer system did not immediately restart. I realized at that moment that there was also a power button on the computer tower that needed to be pressed.

I pushed the button on the tower and saw a little green light on the portable hard drive begin to blink. It continued to blink for three or four very long minutes before finally ceasing.

I detached the cable from the tower and was relieved to finally be out of that room. I walked out the main door and into the parking lot feeling like the whole world was watching me, but nobody was around. I hurried back up to my own room and sat on the edge of my bed with the hard drive in my hands waiting for Amos.

After about half an hour passed with no word, I decided to go up to Amos's room to hand over the device. Upon opening my door, I looked down at the parking lot and was confused to see a police car pulling out of the parking lot.

A second police car sat parked diagonally across three parking spaces just below me. The door to that car swung open and an officer stepped out. He pointed at me. "Hey, you there! Did you know your downstairs neighbor, June?"

"Yeah," I said slowly, wondering what all of this could possibly be about.

The officer pressed a button on the radio system attached to his shoulder, tilted his head, and spoke inaudibly into it. He then slowly walked to the stairs and made his way up to me.

"What's going on with June?" I asked. "Is she okay?"

"Was June a friend?"

I didn't like how this officer was speaking about June in the past tense. "Yes. June *is* a friend of mine. What's going on?"

"Can we go in your room and talk for a second?"

"I guess so." I walked back into my room and took a seat on the edge of my bed.

Once he was with me in my room, the officer stopped a few steps in front of me. "We got a call saying the power went out to your building."

"Yeah. Is that a problem?"

"This woman, June. It seems she had a sleeping condition that required her to wear a very special mask. Do you know anything about that mask?"

The pieces to the puzzle came suddenly crashing together for me.

It hadn't even crossed my mind to think June might be inside Olinc at the time I shut down the power. That special mask she wore while inside the system was designed so it couldn't accidentally come off. Whenever she would normally wake up, the mask would still be pumping air until she removed it and turned off the machine.

If there was suddenly no power to the system, she had no way of getting any air. The power must have been off for close to three minutes. I might as well have gone down to her room and smothered her with a pillow.

This was all my fault.

TWENTY-ONE

I slapped one hand over my mouth and stared directly at the officer. "Is June going to be okay?"

"No. I'm afraid not."

I jumped to my feet and grabbed two fistfuls of my own hair. "This can't be. This can't be happening."

"Let's just start with your name, son," he said.

"Miles. Miles Casey."

"Well, Miles, what do you know about her mask? It took the medics some effort to figure out how to get it off her. It was quite unusual for a CPAP mask." He stepped closer to me. "The most unusual thing is that there was a normal CPAP mask and machine on the nightstand on the other side of her bed. Help me out here."

"She ... two different masks. One for sleeping." I didn't have any idea what to say, or even if I should say anything at all. "She has a special mask for when she was in deep sleep. Designed to not come off by accident."

He looked at me, obviously not convinced I was telling him everything I knew. "What is the machine in her room next to the bed?"

"Her special CPAP machine. For deep sleep."

"Not that one. The other one. There was a single wire coming from the machine and it was connected to the back of her neck. What was that about? Was it monitoring her vitals while she slept? What was it?"

"Something like that."

"You obviously know what it is." He pointed at the machine next to my bed with its wire hanging down. "You have one exactly like it."

"Do I ... do I need a lawyer or something?"

"Look. I don't think you've done anything wrong." He reached into his breast pocket and pulled out a card. He held it out to me. "Here's my number. The second you ask if you need to talk to a lawyer is the second I can't speak to you anymore without a lawyer present."

"So ... do I need a lawyer?" I repeated.

"Like I said, I can't talk to you without a lawyer," he said, pointing again at the card in my hand. "If you want to talk to me, you give me a call or come down to the station. Right now, it's all voluntary. I've got no reason to think you've done anything at all, but I've got a feeling I need to figure out what that machine is. If that machine has anything to do with making Miss June unable to take her mask off, then whoever is responsible for that machine will be held responsible for Miss June."

He stood there, studying my reaction. I could tell by the look in his eye that I had done a terrible job hiding the fact that I knew who had created that machine. I had never bothered to ask anyone who built it, and although I doubted Subi was the one who manufactured it, I was certain she was the brains behind its design.

He scrutinized me for a good twenty seconds before turning toward the door. "If you know something, you're going to want to get out in front of this," he said with his back toward me and then closed it behind him.

What a nightmare. I hadn't wanted to be part of any of this. I hadn't wanted anything to do with the hard drive, or with Amos's crazy ideas, or any of this. Was this my reward for trying to be loyal to everyone on the team?

I peeked out my front door to see if the cop car was still in the parking lot. Since it was just pulling away, I stepped out.

I ran down the stairs to Subi's house and knocked on her door, but nobody answered.

I hurried next door to Z's place because he was likely the best equipped to handle situations that had spun out of control.

Wasn't everyone always saying he had some unusual ability to get people to see things his way and do things for him? Surely, he would be able to strategize, and we could work our way out of this one together. After all, I was the one to pull the plug on the power, but the Olinc company was responsible for the machine.

As I knocked on Z's door, I found myself looking around as if someone was watching me and would notice just how nervous and suspicious I looked. Unfortunately, just like at Subi's door, nobody answered.

I knew I couldn't handle this alone, so I had to settle for the only person left on my list. I hurried up to the top floor of the hotel and knocked on Amos's door.

"What did you just get me to do?!" I said quietly but sternly as I busted into his room.

He was standing in the open doorway to his balcony. "Whoa there, boy. Calm down. Did everything go as planned? Where is the hard drive?"

"There's your hard drive." I tossed it onto the bed. "No. Things did not go as planned. June is dead because of me. Because of you!"

"Slow down. Why is she dead? I never did anything to June."

"When I was rebooting the system, I shut the power down for a few minutes. She wears this mask that doesn't come off. She suffocated."

"Oh yeah? She suffocated?"

There was something about the way he said those last words that made the hair on the back of my neck stand up. I had expected him to be as shocked as I had been, but he wasn't. He only looked like he was trying to pretend he was surprised, but he was as bad at acting as I was.

"When you told me to shut everything down, I didn't realize you meant the whole building. I thought it would just shut down the system."

"Nobody told you to shut the whole building down."

"Of course you did. That's exactly what you told me to do." Something about his demeanor was very unsettling. "I'm starting to wonder if you knew this would happen."

"I did nothing of the sort," he shot back. His posture was changing now. He looked ready to fight back.

"And you knew June was inside the system. She wouldn't normally be in the system so early in the morning, but somehow you knew she was in there."

"What are you trying to say, boy? Are you accusing me of something? You better choose your words very carefully right now." He pointed a finger in my general direction. "Say it!"

"Somebody called in a tip to the police that June was dead. Up until now I couldn't think of who might even realize so quickly that anything happened to her. There would be no way of knowing ..." My voice trailed off for a second as I processed my thoughts. "... Unless someone knew beforehand that she was plugging in. Maybe someone even reached out to invite her in."

"That is quite the accusation, boy. Quite the theory." He relaxed his posture before stepping out onto his balcony. "Something tells me you are going to have a hard time proving any of this to anybody. The only thing the cops are worried about right now is figuring out who is responsible for these machines. We all know who is responsible for them, and it is not you or me. Z and your girlfriend are going down."

I watched him jump up to sit on his railing, and then he swung his legs over one at a time. He pulled his cigarettes from his pocket and stuck one in his mouth.

The only thing I could think of, as I stood there silently staring at his back, was that I wished a big gust of wind would come right now to knock him off balance.

Fuming, I slammed the door behind me on the way out of his room.

I looked up just in time to see Z arriving at his place, so I hurried down the stairs and ran across the parking lot. After knocking, I heard his voice through the door beckon me to come on in without coming to the door himself. As I stepped through the threshold, I realized that I had never actually been inside his house before.

Once I was a step inside his living room, I began spilling every detail of the morning as quickly as I could get it out. I held nothing back. I didn't try to sugarcoat how stupid I felt for shutting down the whole building instead of just the computer tower when I was trying to shut down the system.

"The cop is going to come back. He's going to come poking around again," I said. "What do we tell him?"

"Take a seat, Miles," he said, pointing at a chair that was pushed up next to a square table.

I walked to the table and sat down. He disappeared into the next room and reappeared with a single sheet of paper. He placed it on the table in front of me. It had four single-spaced typed paragraphs on it along with four signatures on the bottom. One signature clearly read Summer Bishop, and next to hers was his own. The other two signatures were names I didn't recognize.

"Do you know why we chose Lincoln City, Oregon for this experiment?" he asked.

"No. Not really. I just assumed you guys liked it because it's a small town, and it's beautiful."

"You're not wrong. Subi used to come here on vacation with her father when she was a little girl. We chose this place partly because she has such fond memories of being here, and she knew she would need to be here for a very long time to oversee operations here." He spun the paper around in front of himself and scanned the names. "The other reason we chose this beautiful little spot on the coast was because I sat down and had a nice long chat with the brass at the police station. That officer who came by this morning is nobody important." He tapped the names on the paper. "These two names are the ones that are important."

"I don't understand. What did you agree to?"

"They know exactly what Olinc is. No secrets," he said. "I told them all about how we plan to help people like June, and how we plan to help people like you and Amos."

For a quick second, I couldn't figure out why he was lumping me in with Amos. I wasn't blind. Then I remembered that I was first recruited for this experiment because he saw me as a troublemaker.

"You've done well for yourself," he said. "Subi and I both trust you completely. We are proud of what you have been able to accomplish."

"Hopefully that helps the way they all see Olinc, then?" I said, more as a question than as a statement.

"That's the hope." He paused and looked me up and down. "What do you think of Olinc? I mean, what do you *really* think of it? You said a while back that you weren't that impressed, and you gave a bunch of reasons why you didn't think people would want to be part of it."

I felt embarrassed at that statement. I had forgotten that I had ever said any of those things.

"Truth is, I think this place does a lot of good," I said. "This place is a miracle for people like June. And I even see the potential of it helping to reform some criminals. I think you need a bit more for it to work with the criminals. Maybe you could have more service opportunities outside of just building the Olinc world ... But yeah. I think this place is amazing."

"What would you think if it all went away?" he said and swiped his hand through the air as if he were wiping it out of existence.

"I think that would be a real shame."

"How big of a shame? A shame—like your pickup truck is never going to run again? That kind of a shame? Or, a shame like it would be life-changing and devastating—that kind of a shame?"

I thought about it for a second or two before responding. "Devastating."

"Me too. And I'm not just saying that because I have so much time and money invested in the system. This thing we have got going here changes the world for the better. It gives people a whole new chance at life. This system means everything to those who get a chance to be part of it."

"I agree."

"Then you agree it needs to be protected at any cost."

"Yes," I agreed before I even knew what I was saying. "Wait, what do you mean—at any cost?"

"You tell me. What is more important than changing people's lives? You tell me what it means to protect this thing at any cost. It's bigger than you. It's bigger than I am. It's bigger than all of us put together."

He leaned back in his chair and folded his arms. "I'll tell you one thing, though. Amos thinks he has us all in checkmate. And he does ... if we can't figure out a way to erase him from the equation."

"Why? I don't understand. What has he got on you?"

"He knows a lot more than we all thought he did. He has obviously been planning this for a long time. He had us all fooled that he didn't want anything to do with Olinc, when in reality he was conniving this plan to take Olinc for himself."

"He played me," I said under my breath.

"He played all of us." Z closed his eyes and gritted his teeth.

"Do you think he had June die on purpose?"

"I do," he said with an angry quiver in his voice. "I think he never had any interest in whatever data you could collect on that hard drive. I think his whole plan was centered around June. With her dead, the police are going to pin manslaughter on Subi and me, if not reckless homicide. Subi and I are going to go down for this while it was actually him committing first-degree murder." He shook his head and covered his face with his hands. "Subi and I will be locked up for years, and with us out of the picture, there will be nothing we can do to keep Amos from taking over everything. He won't have to steal our secrets to build his own version of Olinc if he can just take the whole thing over. He will turn Olinc into whatever he wants it to be. Can you imagine what Amos's world would look like if he were in charge with no moral restrictions attached to it?"

I shuddered at the thought.

The idea of a horrible man premeditating the murder of one of my friends and then pinning it on someone like Subi made me so upset that my mind began to go to dark places it had never been before.

I gritted my teeth and walked out the door. I paced the parking lot as I pondered what I should do, and asked myself what lengths I would go to save Subi, Z, and Olinc. Although I was the lowest man on the Olinc totem pole and had the least amount of power or ability, I felt like this was largely my fault. There had to be something I could do.

That police officer who had visited me in my room immediately began focusing on the machine that connected us to Olinc. I couldn't think of any possible way I could take their attention off that, and that focus would always lead right to Subi and Z.

Hopefully that piece of paper Z had shown me with the four signatures would help protect them from serious charges. Either way, the idea that Amos could get away with his plan and then walk away was out of the question.

As I ran through different scenarios of how to stop him, I planted my feet and looked straight up into the gray Oregon sky. Tiny droplets of rain and mist were beginning to fall. I repeatedly blinked my eyes as the cold bits of sky fell down on me.

I knew what I was going to do. Every other option I tried to conjure up would simply not work. I closed my eyes and tried to talk myself out of this decision because of the incredible chance I was about to take, but it had to be done. So many things could go wrong, but the risk was worth it.

TWENTY-TWO

I stood just outside Amos's door working up my courage. I hated the fact that I had been pulled into this. Last year at this time my life was so incredibly boring. The biggest drama that happened in my life that year was watching the Seattle Mariners get close to making the playoffs and still somehow lose the last game of the season, disqualifying them from the tournament.

Looking back at the last five months, I could see every step that led me here, but none of those steps felt like a problem in the moment.

I had never been in any type of situation that even compared to this before. As nervous as I was, I felt I had no other option.

I didn't knock on Amos's door. I just took a deep breath and quietly twisted the doorknob. I opened the door slowly and found him right where I had left him—sitting on the edge of the railing on his balcony.

The sliding glass door was still open.

I stood there watching him as he calmly brought his left hand up to his mouth to steal a puff of smoke from the little white stick between his fingers before bringing his hand back down again. His right hand rested comfortably on his lap. He wasn't even trying to hold on.

I stepped quietly across the room toward the open glass door of his balcony and then stopped. I stood there just behind him for what felt like an eternity.

This was a turning point in my life.

"Are you just going to stand there, or are you going to say something?" Amos said without turning around.

"I just—" I didn't know what to say.

"Yeah. You are not as sneaky as you think you are."

"What now?"

"You tell me. You're the one who needs to clean up this mess."

"I'm not the one who killed June."

"We both know that's not true." He laughed. "You were the one who turned off the power. She choked when the power went off. Seems to me you are the only one responsible. You, and your girlfriend."

"You tricked me into turning the power off. I didn't know that was going to happen."

"So?"

"Why did you want June dead? She was the nicest lady in the world. Even you knew that."

"Casualties are a part of war."

"War!? Nobody's at war!"

"Maybe you're not, but my entire life has always been a war. Me against the world. That is how it has always been in the past. That is how it still is today."

"You didn't have to kill June. You're going to have to answer for that."

"Good luck pinning that on me. What evidence do you have? It seems to me there is only one piece of physical evidence." He took a drag from his cigarette before lowering his arm back down. "And that evidence is not going to help you one bit."

He stumped me on that one. "What are you talking about?"

"The hard drive. It has your fingerprints all over it."

"How did the cops get the hard drive?"

He turned his head halfway toward me. "One nosy cop came up here just after you left. He was asking all kinds of questions. I told him I don't know anything about the building being shut down or June suffocating to death. I told him the only thing that seemed unusual about today was when you came barging into my room, threw the hard drive onto the bed, and told me to hide it for you while the cops were snooping around."

"You didn't," I said incredulously.

"I never touched that thing. Never. So, there are fingerprints all over that hard drive, and none of them are mine." He took a drag from his cigarette and let the smoke escape through his nostrils. "Yes. It is your word against mine. Good luck with that."

I thought back to when I first got the drive from him. It was true. I never saw the drive in his hand. He directed me to his nightstand where I opened the drawer and took it out myself. He never handed it to me. When I made it back to the room, I just tossed it onto his bed.

"You killed June," I said as my blood began to boil.

"So? What are you going to do about it?"

"You killed June. That doesn't bother you?"

"She was in the way. Now she is out of the way. Now nothing is in the way for me to take over Olinc."

I'd had enough of this conversation. I was so angry that my hands were balled into fists, and I was about to shatter my own teeth from clenching my jaw so hard.

I turned on my heel and stormed out of there, slamming the front door.

I walked down to my pickup truck and slid into the driver's seat. I pulled the keys out of my pocket but just held them in my hand. I leaned forward and rested my forehead on the steering wheel for a few minutes as I gathered myself.

When I sat up and looked around at the tall hotel building, then at the main entrance building, and then at Subi and Z's houses across the street, I couldn't help but wonder if this was the end of it all. It certainly felt like it was the end of my tenure here, but I couldn't help but wonder if it was also the end of Olinc as I knew it.

All I could do was play the cards I was dealt and hope for the best.

I pulled my cell phone from my pocket and asked it to give me the address for the Lincoln City police station. When the address and directions appeared on my screen, I slid my key into the ignition and brought the engine to life.

The drive to the station was only a few miles, but it felt farther than driving to the Redwoods.

Once I reached the front desk, I pulled the business card from my pocket and asked for the officer I had spoken to earlier. A lady escorted me to a room where I sat alone in my thoughts—thoughts that questioned every decision I had made over the last six months. All of this started when I jumped into Jason's car at the stoplight and was too dumb to realize what he was up to. If I had just called a cab to come pick me up like everyone else in the world would have done, I would still be sitting at home right now with a bucket of popcorn and watching old reruns of *Law & Order* rather than being the subject of it.

The door eventually opened, but the officer who entered was not the officer who had given me his card earlier in the day. I knew him, though. This was Officer McKnight. He was the same man who had approached me months ago as I walked the beach and asked me how everyone was treating me.

"Miles Casey," he said with a subdued smile. "You're in a bit of a bind, aren't you?"

There was something about the look in his eye. It made me wonder if he knew this day would come—like he had tried to warn me about this months ago. But he wasn't wearing an I-told-you-so expression. Rather, it was one of empathy.

I pulled my cell phone from my pocket and laid it on the table. "What do you know about what's been going on at our hotel today?"

"I think I have a pretty full picture." He took a seat directly across from me at the table.

I turned my phone on and pressed a few buttons. "I don't know what the laws are in Oregon about recording other people without their permission. I don't know whether this will be admissible in court or anything, but you need to hear this."

I pressed play on my phone. Prior to this moment, I had thought the worst-case scenario would be that the audio might be too muffled to understand. The phone had been in my pocket the whole time I recorded my conversation with Amos, after all.

But the strangest thing happened when I pressed the play button. The officer and I sat there together and listened to the entire five-minute conversation, but there was only one voice on the recording. My own voice came through crystal clear, but Amos's voice was completely absent. I pushed the volume all the way to the top level and held my ear an inch away from the phone to see if I could hear his voice in the distance, but there was nothing at all. It was as if the recording was just of me talking to myself.

There came the moment on the recording when I flat out accused him of killing June, and I remembered very clearly that his only response had been to say, "So? What are you going to do about it?" I closed my eyes and hoped his voice would somehow appear in that moment, but there was only silence. Then I repeated my accusation, followed by more silence.

"I don't get it," I said in a bit of a panic. "I recorded my conversation with Amos just an hour ago. He confessed to everything."

"Take a breath," Officer McKnight said.

"You don't understand. Amos killed June. Not me. It was Amos. He did it," I said as I started the recording over again.

"Whoa. Whoa. Whoa. Take a breath."

"This can't be happening." I said as I held the phone right up against my ear. "I don't know what happened to that recording. He should be on there as clear as day. He spilled everything."

He grabbed both of my hands into his and squeezed, causing me to drop my phone onto the table. I looked up to see him wearing half a smile.

"I believe you."

"You do?" I almost asked him why, but I was afraid I might talk him out of it.

"I know everything. I know more than you do, in fact. I know all about the experiment you have been part of. Pretty cruel, if you ask me."

I didn't like the sound of that. I pulled my hands away and folded my arms across my chest. "What do you mean? Who killed June, then. It was Amos, right?"

He pointed down at my phone. "I assume you have June's phone number in there."

"Yeah."

"Call her."

I looked at him like he was crazy. What part of her being dead did he not understand?

"Call her," he urged again.

I pulled up her number and pressed the call button. I left the phone on speaker mode and kept my eyes glued to the officer as it rang.

"Hey, Miles! What are you up to?" came June's unmistakable voice through the phone.

I continued to stare at the officer for a long time before responding. "June? Are you okay?"

"Yeah." She sounded confused. "How come? Why wouldn't I be?"

"Did you spend time in Olinc this morning?"

"Yes. Most of the morning. How come?"

"Were you inside Olinc when the power went out?"

"No. I was just in my room eating breakfast. I went into Olinc right after. What are all these questions about?"

I breathed a sigh of relief. "I was just worried you were in Olinc when the power went out, and you would have been stuck in your mask."

"Ooh, that would have been bad. We should probably make sure to get a generator for the building or something in case that ever does happen. Or, at least get me a battery pack for my CPAP. Something that will kick on immediately if the power goes out."

We exchanged a few pleasantries and closed the conversation. My mind was swimming now. Knowing that June was perfectly fine was the coolest feeling in the world, but it was mixed with the fire of what the officer had said just before I called June. Whatever this was, whatever had been going on today, was part of the "experiment" I had signed up for nearly six months ago.

The smile on the face of Officer McKnight disappeared as soon as I turned my eyes back on him. My face must have done a good job of expressing exactly what I was thinking and feeling in the moment because he immediately started scrambling for words.

"Look. Yes. Look," he mumbled. "Yes, I've known about this experiment for a long time. I knew about it even before you were selected to be part of it. I never liked it. I thought it was cruel."

"What was the experiment?"

"Ramsey Mir has an unusual fascination with psychology," he said as he leaned away from me. "He wanted to see how far a man could be pushed. If they were to control a whole bunch of variables, could they nudge someone into doing the ultimate action? Could they push someone so far that they would make the decision on their own, and carry it out?"

"What decision?"

"The decision to kill another human being."

"Yeah, well, they succeeded. They tricked me into killing June. Or, at least they made me think I did."

He shook his head. "Not June. Amos."

Now I was confused. I looked around the room as I tried to put together what he had just said. "I didn't kill Amos. Nobody killed Amos."

"You're right. Nobody killed Amos, but that was what they were trying to get you to do. They backed you into a corner. Their goal was to make you think there was no way out."

"Except for me to push Amos off the railing," I concluded.

Officer McKnight nodded. "Cruel. I'm sorry they put you through this."

"But what if I had pushed Amos?" I said, throwing my hands in the air. "I admit it did cross my mind, even though I don't think I ever seriously considered following through with it. If they were to have succeeded with their experiment, then it would have ended with me in prison with a life sentence."

"No." He shook his head. "Amos is not what he seems. If you had pushed him, he would have been just fine."

I didn't know what to say to that. How could he be just fine? A seventy-foot drop onto a concrete ledge would have been plenty of reason for him to not be "just fine."

"Look. I'm sure you have a million questions." He pushed my cell phone back toward me. "The experiment is over. Go home. Talk to them. They can give you better answers than I can."

TWENTY-THREE

I had every intention of going straight home to confront Z when I stepped into my truck, but as I came out of the police station parking lot, I found myself turning south instead. It was as if I were on autopilot. Even I didn't know where I was heading.

A long time ago, when I was a young boy, I ate a banana. Within the hour, while I still had the taste of that banana in my mouth, my stomach began to cramp, and I began to vomit uncontrollably. I was terribly sick for the next forty-eight hours. To this day, I still can't eat bananas. The strangest part of the ordeal was that I still enjoyed the taste, and yet, even just the sight or the smell of a banana was enough to make my insides start to turn. Now, as an adult, I doubted I would ever be able to overcome that aversion, even though I was almost certain the food poisoning had come from something I had eaten earlier and had nothing whatsoever to do with the banana.

I knew every inch of this drive through Lincoln City. As I passed some of my most familiar places, I felt as if I were taking a farewell tour of the Oregon coast. I was going to use this credit card in my pocket to fill up my gas tank and get home, and I didn't know if I would ever be coming back. I loved every inch of this area, but I was certain that, from this day forward, just the sight or the smell of this beautiful area would be enough to make my stomach turn.

As I exited Lincoln City, I found my mind fixated on an area I had passed many times and always told myself I would come back to explore it. I always told myself I needed to experience it so June could have it as one of her meditation spots. That was where I needed to go. Not for June, but for myself.

I didn't like feeling this way. I didn't like how one of my favorite places on earth had turned into something so painful in a matter of just a few minutes. I needed an escape. I needed some "Zen time," as June would say. I needed a moment in a neutral location to allow my mind to work on separating the good from the bad.

South of Lincoln City was the town of Newport, Oregon. Running through the center of Newport was Yaquina Bay. I had been to the area many times. On the north side of the bay were Cobble Beach and the Yaquina Bay Lighthouse where I had spent more time than anywhere else. I had never visited the south side of the bay, though, where there was a jetty about twenty feet wide and thirty feet high that extended for about a mile out into the Pacific Ocean.

The jetty was not intended to be a walking path, and I didn't often see people out on it. Perhaps that was why I felt drawn to it. Nobody would be there.

I drove my truck as far as the road would allow, and then I pressed down on the parking brake. Before stepping out, I realized that behind my seat I still had that silly kite I had purchased once upon a time. I grabbed it and set off on foot.

It didn't take long for sand to begin accumulating inside my tennis shoes, and the wind blasting that same sand into my face stung my skin while making it difficult to see. Closer to shore, the waves would rise and fall from only a few feet. The farther I made it out to sea, though, the waves were much more majestic. They roared as they climbed halfway up both sides of the jetty and smashed into the rocks. It was as if the waves were trying to tell me I didn't belong there, and that they had the power to jump up, grab me, and pull me out to sea if they so chose.

I made it to the end of the jetty and looked back at the town of Newport in the distance. For the moment, the Oregon coast felt far away and I was ... nowhere.

The wind out here was angry. As I held tightly to my kite string, large gusts would come unexpectedly to try to jerk me off my feet. To keep me off balance. To tumble me down the rocks and into the hands of the vast ocean. I was stronger than the winds, though. The longer I stood there, the better I got at leaning into the winds so I wouldn't have to fight against them.

I was as angry at Z as I had ever felt toward anyone in my life. The same went for Amos. I wasn't exactly sure how everything tied together, but I was sure those two were equally to blame for this nightmare.

I had no reason to be upset with June. I was willing to bet she knew even less about this than I did.

It was obvious to me why I was the target. I doubted they would have ever been able to pressure that gentle woman into even smashing a cockroach, let alone take the life of a human being. And as I thought of these things, it became clear to me why Z hadn't wanted to choose me in the first place—why he had said I was "boring." If Jason had been standing there in my shoes within arm's reach of Amos as he sat atop that balcony railing, he would have shoved him off without hesitation. I was certain of that.

The primary question in my mind was Subi.

I pulled harder on the string, and maneuvered the kite left and right. I released more and more length, but the only thing that seemed to change was that the kite felt farther away. I pulled hard and watched the kite rise to its apex, and then I completely let go of the line. The kite lifted up, spun a complete counterclockwise circle in the sky, and then smashed down into the Pacific Ocean.

I shoved my hands into my pockets and looked up at the empty sky.

How much of this mess did Subi know? I got the feeling she and Z had separate agendas throughout this whole ordeal. I had always felt that way, but how much of this would be a surprise? There was no way she could have been a full participant in this brutal experiment. No way.

She sure did carry a lot of secrets, though. I had always thought that those secrets couldn't be too awful. I had always assumed her secrets couldn't be so serious that I would want to write her off and never see her again. There was no way I had misjudged her so badly that she was just as devious and conniving as Z. No way.

I turned around again to look back at the coastline, and I saw a figure in the distance walking toward me atop the jetty. She still had a long way to go before catching up to me, but I knew that figure immediately.

I fought back the urge to meet her halfway and waited patiently for her to come to me.

And there she stood, right in front of me. Her hair blew across her face as the wind swirled furiously around us. She just stared at me for a long time, clearly not knowing what to say or where to start. There was no mistaking the pain I could see in those eyes.

"How did you know I was here?" I asked, even though I already knew the answer.

"Phone tracker," she said, and without skipping a beat she continued with, "I'm so incredibly sorry. I had no idea what Amos and Z were up to. No idea."

"Who is Amos, really? I get the feeling he wasn't just some guy you pulled out of jail like I was."

"The simple answer is that Amos is someone Z and I have known for many years. Amos lives in Idaho with everyone else."

"Okay. That's the simple answer. Now, what's the full answer?"

She paused for a moment before nodding. "Let's take a step back. Way back. And feel free to stop me at any time to ask any questions you might have. No more secrets."

"No more secrets," I agreed.

She pointed to the spot just behind her ear. "The implant. I think you know basically how it works. As you look around, as you smell things, taste things, hear things, feel things—as you use your senses to experience the world around you, the implant collects all that data. That's how the world of Olinc is being built. You already know all of this."

"Yes."

"What you may not fully understand, is that the implant is reading a lot of other things your brain does too. It doesn't have the power to read your thoughts, of course, that would be impossible, but—" she paused, clearly not quite sure how to explain this. "Do you know how a lie detector test works? They hook you up with a bunch of wires that read your pulse, your breathing, and your blood pressure, all those kinds of things. A lie detector reads the way your body changes when you are speaking, and it can tell by your physiology whether you feel a certain way about what you're saying. Whether or not you're lying."

"My chip is reading all those things. Probably more than just those things."

"A lot more. Every scenario you were in, whether that be just lounging around the house, to being scared, or nervous, or excited, or any emotion you can imagine—the chip reads all the signals your body sends to your brain."

I didn't like where this was going at all. "You had me get close to you so my chip could read all those emotions? Is that why you kissed me? Did your father even pass away?"

Her mouth dropped open, and a look of panic flashed through her eyes. "No. No. No. Please don't think anything like that." She grabbed my right hand with both of hers and held it close to her chest. "I would never even think to use you like that. Everything I ever felt for you is real. Everything."

I gently pulled my hand away and slid it back into my pocket. "You'll forgive me if I say my jury is still deliberating."

"That's fair."

I walked a few feet away and sat on the edge of an enormous boulder. "So, what do you and the team plan to do with all the data you collect from my brain?" I tapped the tip of my index finger onto the side of my head. "What good does it do you to know how I feel when I kiss a girl or when I'm tempted to shove an evil man off a balcony?"

She sat down next to me. "The chip reads all your reactions to everything. As the months go by, as it collects more and more about you, then the system begins to read you in a way that it can predict what you're going to feel even before you react. Through time, it can predict what you would say in any given conversation. What you would do. Five months is not enough time to know everything about you, but it can gather quite a bit. In essence, the system knows you so well that it could create a mirror image of you."

I looked at her sideways. "You plan to make a mirror image of me? A doppelganger? A copy of me? And I suppose you're going to let that faux Miles run free inside Olinc for other people to interact with?"

"Not quite, but you are on the right track. We don't have any plans to create a mirror image of you. That was not why we brought you aboard." She pulled her hair out of her face, but the wind immediately blew it right back. She looked up at me. "The reason we needed you for the experiment was that we needed someone who had no idea any of this was even a possibility. We needed to know if someone could fully interact with a mirror image and never suspect anything was off. To never suspect there was anything different about them at all."

"But I didn't see anyone at all when I was inside Olinc."

"Not just inside Olinc. There are certain parts of the system that are visible on both sides of the line. When you are connected to the wire, you are fully immersed in that world, but when you are not connected, there are only some things you would see, or hear, or experience. There are some things that exist in both worlds."

"Wait. Wait. Wait." I slapped my hand over my eyes. I couldn't help but feel a little dumb at this revelation. "You're telling me I've been talking to someone this whole time who was a mirror image. Someone who exists only in the system? Someone who wasn't really there?"

She said nothing, which confirmed my interpretation.

"Amos," I said almost under my breath. "When I played back the recording, my voice was the only voice on it. The cop at the station told me that if I had pushed Amos over the balcony, he would have been just fine. This whole time I was talking to Amos, he wasn't real." Then I realized something very strange. "Hold on. If I would have tried to push him off that railing, my hands would have gone right through him because he wasn't real."

"You very much would have been able to push him off the balcony, and he very much would have hit the concrete ledge down below just like anyone else." She shook her head. "This is going to be hard for you to do but try to adjust what you mean by the word 'real.' If you see something, and you can touch something, and if that something can think and act independently from anything you might want it to do, then I contend it is real. The mirror image of Amos may not be real to the average person walking down the street, but he was completely real to you. Not only could you talk to him, but you could touch him, and he could touch you. And, yes, you could shove him off a balcony."

My brain felt like it was about to pop now. "How is it possible I was never able to figure that out. I'm such a fool."

"Miles, I need to tell you something more."

"I mean, seriously. Z wanted me to spend all that time getting to know Amos and I thought I was working on getting him to link up to Olinc, and—"

"Miles—" she tried to interrupt me.

"But this whole time you guys were just trying to see, even after all that time I spent with Amos if—"

"Miles." She placed one hand on my cheek and turned my face toward her. "I'm trying to tell you that I'm real."

What a strange thing for her to say. It took me a second to register what she was actually trying to tell me.

"I have my own thoughts, and ideas, and feelings," she said. "Everything I have felt for you is genuine, and it is real. *I* am real."

"But you are—" I couldn't quite finish my sentence.

"I'm real. Just not in the way you have naturally assumed for the last five months."

TWENTY-FOUR

I stood thirty feet away from Subi and watched her for the longest time. When I had first jumped up and walked away, she had also risen to her feet and pleaded with me to come sit back down to hear her out.

I had never been such a mess of emotions. I felt like such a sucker. I felt like I had fallen for a horribly insensitive joke, and there was probably a long list of people in Idaho laughing it up right now. I was half lab rat and half punchline.

On the other hand, I'd had conversations with AI on the internet countless times in the past. Every time I needed instructions on how to fix my truck or build something in the garage, I conversed with AI. Just about every time I called customer service to pay a bill or to ask for some form of assistance, it wasn't hard to tell I wasn't talking to a real person. Artificial intelligence was everywhere in my life. This was not the same thing. Not only had I never suspected anything of the sort regarding Subi, but I had held her in my arms. I had felt her fingertips tickle my forearm as we watched a movie. She had kissed me in a way that was so real, so heartfelt, that it surpassed any kiss I had ever experienced before.

Subi was still on her feet, but she was squatting down now into a ball with her arms wrapped around her legs and her right cheek atop her knees. With her back to me, I couldn't see the tears, but it was not hard to tell by the way she was breathing that this was an intense cry.

What did that even mean? Only people cry from being emotional. I had seen animals be sad before, but I had never seen tears. Plants didn't cry. Robots didn't cry. Only people did that.

Even the AI figures I had seen and interacted with many times in the past were so obvious in their programming that I always knew instinctively that they were not like me. None of these things would have ever been able to fool me into thinking they were real.

Subi was none of those things.

If a robot were to come after me to hurt me, I wouldn't hesitate to smash it with a hammer. Even if it were made to look and feel and interact just like a human, I wouldn't think twice about destroying it. Why was that? It would be because I wouldn't have the slightest emotional connection to it like I would have with a person. That was why.

I had that with Subi, though. I had that in spades. I could never just up and hurt her. That option did not even exist for me. Just the fact that she was curled up right now in emotional agony was tearing me apart. Why was that?

There was only one reason I could think of.

Subi was real.

Like she had said, maybe she wasn't real in quite the same way I had assumed, but she was real. Her touch was real. The way we interacted was unique to us, genuine, interesting, personal, and real. She looked real. She sounded real.

Subi was real.

I walked over to her and stood right next to her for a while before sitting down again. I folded my hands into my lap and looked out over the ocean.

She turned her head away from me.

"I wish I knew what to say, or even how to react," I said. "This is a lot to process."

"I knew it would be," she sniffled and turned her face back toward me. She unwrapped her arms from around her legs and stood up. "I think I'm ready to head back home. Stay here as long as you need." She began to walk away.

"How did you get here?" I brushed off my pants and began to follow after her. "Did you have the system drop you off here? Did you take a cab?"

"June drove me here. Normally I would have ordered a cab but I needed someone to talk to. She's waiting for me in her car close to where you parked."

"Couldn't you just tell the Olinc system to drop you off here? Why would you need to order a cab or have someone drive you?"

"I can see why you would think that. In your mind I am just something digital, and digital things don't have the limitations you might have, but I do have those same limitations. In my world, I can't just teleport or pop in and out of places. I have to travel around just like you do to get from here to there."

"You just called it *your* world. Why did you call it your world? You obviously live in this world too. You're here right now."

"But I'm not in your world. Not really." She shook her head. "Olinc is my world. Even right now, the only things I can see are the parts of Olinc that have been mapped out."

"You don't have to plug into your Olinc machine to be in Olinc?"

"I've never had to plug in because I never leave Olinc. The only reason you can see me is because you have that special chip." She tapped her finger to the space just behind her ear.

"You're seriously inside Olinc right now? How is it you are able to be here with me right now, then? I've never mapped out this place before. This whole area should be that white void we experienced once when we drove past the limits of Olinc. If you and I were to jump in my truck right now and I drove you out past the areas I've mapped out, then all you would see is nothingness while I see the normal world. Isn't that right?"

"No. Not with you. You see, you're growing the Olinc map right now in real time," she said, pointing around. "You have the special mapping chip in your brain, so if I'm traveling with you, then wherever you go, I am able to see what you see because you are constantly giving new input to the system. If I were to begin walking right now and I were to walk off in that direction," she said, raising a finger in the direction of the city of Newport, "then after a few miles I would find the edge of Olinc and I would walk into the void. But if you were with me, we could just keep driving and driving indefinitely and I would see the same things you see. It wouldn't have as much detail to it compared to if you had made the drive multiple times, but my world would grow along with your observations."

I stared at her as my brain tried to process the complexity of the situation. "I can drive you back to Lincoln City," I eventually said.

"June is already here. She's waiting for me."

I grabbed her wrist gently and turned her toward me. "Unless you really don't want to, I'd like to drive you back."

She studied me for a moment. "Okay. You've got a million questions. I guess I owe you a million answers." She pulled out her cell phone and tapped the screen with her thumbs before sliding it back into her pocket. "Done. I sent her home."

"So, you can't drive a car in my world, but you can ride in a car ..." I said, trying to put more pieces of the puzzle together.

"In your world, nobody can see me except you and June."

"And Z and Amos, you mean, right? Everyone except me, and June, and Amos, and Z?"

She only gave me a half smile in response.

"Of course they are. All three of you are mirror images. You. Amos. Z."

"As I was saying," she continued, "I'm invisible to everyone else in your world except you and June, and a handful of people back home in Idaho who work for the company and have the chip. Your chip makes it so you can see me whether you're plugged into the system or not, and I can see you at all times too, whether you're in your world or plugged into mine. Everyone else in the world is invisible to me. The only people I see are those who have a chip. Does that make sense?"

"What about physical objects? You and I sat together on the sofa, and we wrapped ourselves in a blanket. Was it just in my head that I was feeling a blanket?"

"Amos, Z, and I aren't the only things you can see in both worlds. I have to go into the program and specifically add things to the list, but I can make things visible to you in both worlds," she said. "There really is furniture in my house that you can sit on. Anyone in your world could walk into my house right now and sit on my sofa, but there are some things that only exist inside Olinc."

"Like the blanket you had on your couch?"

"Right. Like the blanket I had on my couch," she repeated, and then she started holding up her fingers one-by-one as she made a list. "Your pickup truck. Furnishings in and around the hotel. The Harley-Davidson motorcycle ..."

This made sense, but it sure made my head spin. "What about you moving physical objects? How is it you can interact with things in my world? I've seen you move things, haven't I? I would have noticed otherwise."

"No. I can't move anything in your world. Ever since you got here, Amos, Z, and I have been very careful about the things we've touched. If you think about it, Amos probably looked at the motorcycles at the Harley-Davidson store, but he wouldn't have been able to move one. I've always wondered if you ever realized that we literally live on the beach, but you and I have never walked the beaches together unless you were plugged into Olinc. That's because, in your eyes, you would be leaving footprints, but I wouldn't."

"What would happen if I tried to smoke one of Amos's cigarettes? I could see those whether I was plugged in or not."

"You could smoke one of his cigarettes. Sure. Your brain would even tell your body to feel the sensation of the smoke in your lungs and on your taste buds. It would feel just the same to you as smoking one in the real world."

"That's wild." My mind began racing through every interaction I could come up with that had happened since I woke up in Lincoln City. My mind bounced back and forth between feeling like such a dupe, and marveling at the complex beauty of it all.

"Let me broaden your understanding a little more," she said. "Do you remember back when you were new to Lincoln City and we explained to you how the system works? One example we gave you was that if you were to go to the grocery store inside Olinc and you were to take a gallon of milk from the dairy section, then that spot on the milk rack would remain empty until you, or someone else with the mapping chip, were to look at that rack in your world. As soon as you observe the dairy section in the real world, then everything you saw would update in real time and there would be milk back on that shelf again."

"Sure. I remember that."

"Well, I live inside Olinc at all times. I never leave. If I'm walking around the store alone, I can grab that gallon of milk," she said. "But what do you think happens if I am with you and you are looking at that gallon of milk when I try to grab it."

I pondered the thought for a moment, and then shook my head saying, "I don't know."

"If you are looking at that gallon of milk, then that gallon of milk is perpetually updating itself to be right there! I can't move it while you are looking at it. But if you turn your back and you aren't observing that milk anymore, I would be able to pick it up just fine ... unless you turn back around again."

"What happens if I turn back around and you are holding the gallon of milk?"

"As soon as you see that milk in the real world, then your chip updates everything instantaneously, telling the system the milk is on the shelf and not in my hands. The milk would disappear from my hands and be right back on the shelf."

I stared at her for a long time as my mind tried to wrap itself around this new concept.

"Here." She pointed to a rock on the ground. "I can see that little black rock right there because you have seen it, which has made it part of my world. If you are not looking at it, I can pick up that rock because it is just a regular part of my world. If I'm with you and you are looking at it—" She leaned over to pick it up. I expected to see her hand go right through it like she was a ghost or something, but instead her fingers wrapped around it, and it was as if it was glued to the ground. "You see? Your eyes and your chip update things in real time. If you turn your back, then I can pick it up like normal."

"But as soon as I turn back around and look at the rock again, it would disappear from your hand and be right back where I last saw it," I surmised.

She nodded.

I bent down and picked up the same rock. It was about the same size and weight as a golf ball. I asked her to hold out her hand. When she did so, I held it about six inches above her open palm and then dropped it. The rock knocked her hand out of the way as if it weighed a thousand pounds. It then bounced off the sand and rolled a few inches just like I expected it to. I stared at the rock for about ten seconds before continuing with, "Doors. What about doors? How do you walk through doors?"

"Doors are tricky, for sure. When I'm alone, I just open the door like normal because I am only interacting with my world. But when I'm with you, I have to wait for you to open the door."

I slapped the palm of my hand to my forehead. "I always thought it was just a funny quirk that all of you have. You, Amos, Z. None of you ever answer the door for me. You always just yell for me to come on in."

She gave me a genuine smile. "That's why I always had you open my door for me everywhere we went, including with your pickup truck. I bet you just thought I was very traditional, always expecting the gentleman to open the door for the lady."

The top of the jetty where we were walking was mostly rocks and sand. Because of this, it would be easy to twist an ankle. I kept my eyes on the ground as we walked, and for the first time since I was with her, I noticed the difference in our footsteps. Under my feet, I left a chevron-style imprint of size eleven tennis shoes. Under her feet, however, there were no prints at all.

As we were approaching my truck, my mind tried to process the various nuances of what I had just learned. I looked out at the water and wondered what would happen if she were to step out onto the ocean.

Would it be just like the sand where she wouldn't sink into it at all? Could she walk on the water, or would she sink to the bottom like my brain would expect her to in the real world? As curious as I was, I felt like our deep-hearted conversation was already awkward enough that I figured those questions could wait for another day.

Once we reached my truck, I made sure to open the door for her. She gave me a smile and climbed in. I took one step away before I remembered I needed to close it for her.

Once we were on our way back toward Lincoln City, there were a lot of breaks in the conversation as I sifted through my thoughts. Every so often, I would take my eyes off the road to look over at her. I felt my heart pulled in two different directions.

I was reminded of years ago when I was inside this same pickup truck with my high school girlfriend. There came a day when she made the decision to move away to begin a new life in a new town. When I began to express a desire to relocate along with her, the image of her shaking her head became imprinted forever in my memory as she said, "What I'm trying to tell you is that I am ready to move on without you."

This felt similar, and yet, it was completely different. The hurt was similar, but what made this even worse was that, not only did I want to be with her, but I knew she equally wanted to be with me. It wasn't any lack of feeling for one another that would keep us apart, but this had to be the end of the line for us. Subi had warned me that this would happen, but I lacked the ability to understand why that would be necessary.

For most of our time on the road, I had been failing to build up the courage to ask my biggest question. It was obvious it needed to be asked, and part of me was hoping she would address it without me having to be the one to bring it up.

"Why did you let things get this far?" I finally asked once we were halfway through Lincoln City.

This brought the tears back to her eyes—tears that I was sure were already just below the surface.

"Do you mean, why did I do this to you?" she sniffled. "Or are you asking why I did this to myself?"

I thought for a few seconds before responding. "Both."

"For my side, the answer is easy. In the beginning, I needed a friend. Like I said months ago, I was lonely for a friend. I needed someone besides June because she is more like a mother figure to me, and someone besides Z who is ... well, he's just Z." She turned her whole body toward me, placing one arm on the back of the seat and the other hand on the dashboard. "I fell in love with you."

This sent all kinds of emotions charging through me like a rodeo bull being let loose inside the china shop of my mind.

"I woke up every morning and had to ask myself what on earth I thought I was doing—letting things go on and on like this," she said. "Knowing that the more I went down this road, the more it would hurt when it came to its inevitable end. The closer we came to ... today." She paused and looked out at the road again for a long time before continuing. "The closer we came to losing my dad, the more his body was shutting down, the more I thought about him and the more it hurt. I thought about him every second of every day in the end. I still do. And as I thought about him, I could hear his voice inside my head repeating those words, 'Fall in love with someone who, when the worst day of your life comes, he is the one you need and want there with you.' You were that for me. You were there for me on my worst day. I needed you and I wanted you there. You were worth it to me. All the hurt I knew I was in for, and everything I'm feeling today ... you were worth the hurt."

The bull in my brain smashed a vase, and then an entire set of expensive dinnerware.

She turned back in her seat to where she was again facing forward. "But then there's the question about how I could do this to you," she said softly. "If I truly cared about you, why would I set you up like this? Am I really that selfish?" She took a deep breath. "In a way, yes. I guess I am selfish in that way."

Smash! There went a beautiful lamp. *Crash!* And there went another antique vase.

She folded her hands into her lap and lowered her chin to her chest. "I knew I was gambling with your heart. I knew that. And for that, I'm so very sorry." She looked over at me. "I could say that I wasn't allowed to tell you because Z and I had made the decision long ago that we wouldn't tell you everything until the experiment was over. I could say those kinds of things, but in reality, I'm a big girl. I helped make the rules. I could have broken them if I wanted to, and Z could have done nothing about it."

"But you let me fall in love with you anyway."

"I did because I love you. I did because I wanted you to love me just as much. I wanted you to love me so much that you didn't want this to end after I had to tell you all these things."

"Subi, I—" I didn't even know what to say to that. All my feelings I'd had toward her were real, and they were genuine, but the idea of staying with her was just not an option.

"I don't mean that I want you to stay here in Lincoln City. It's time for you to move on. I know that. You need to go back to Idaho." She took in a deep breath. "What I mean, is that I am back in Idaho also. There is a part of me there too."

"You're hoping I will go back to Idaho and convince the Idaho version of you to fall in love with me. The version of you that is—" I didn't want to say Subi wasn't real. That would have seemed insulting to her, and it didn't feel accurate. "The version of you that is ... just like me."

"Summer. People call me Subi, and they call her Summer. To me, we are one and the same. She is me, and I am her, but for communication purposes, it helps other people to call us different names."

"What do you mean you are the same? You're clearly separate beings."

"But we're not separate. With everything she is going through, just like with you, all that data is collected in real time. Every bit of emotion, every memory, everything she experiences ... those are all part of me too. When Dad died, Summer was right there at his bedside. I can picture it in my mind because I have that memory, and I received it in real time. I didn't need someone to text me a message to let me know when he passed away because I was there when it happened. I was in my Lincoln City living room with you, and I was at my father's bedside—both at the same time."

"But Idaho Subi—" I stopped to correct myself. "I mean, Summer doesn't receive any memories or emotions from you."

"Yes. That's right."

"You kissed me because you love me," I continued, "but she doesn't have those feelings, does she? I've only met her once, and I was in a county jail jumpsuit at the time."

She made a face that said my words weren't entirely true. "Well, you actually talked with her one day while you were here. Summer sat directly in front of you during your first team meeting. She was in town that day."

"I remember. She ... you ... she ... was wearing your wedding ring," I said. "That was kind of an awkward meeting because of the way she looked at me differently. She had no feelings for me whatsoever. Not even as a friend."

"She is me, and I am her. I know how she thinks. I know what she feels. I know what she wants. And I know what she needs. I know you think of the two of us as separate entities, but we aren't."

I pulled the truck into the parking lot and brought it to a stop in my usual parking space by the stairs. I slipped the keys out of the ignition and then looked at them in my hand. I didn't look up until I felt her hand gently on my forearm.

"I'm coming to you like a little schoolgirl again," she said. "I'm asking you to catch me all over again. I'm asking you to let Summer fall in love with you. I know she will come to love you just the same as I have because we fit together so perfectly. As it happens, every memory and emotion will be part of me all over again."

"Like a schoolgirl?" I smiled. "Check yes or no."

She smiled back. "Check yes or no."

TWENTY-FIVE

Relationships always needed to be balanced. If I were to go back to Idaho and ask Summer on a date, there would be no balance between us because I was already in love with her and she didn't know me at all. I would be starting over with my efforts while my heart was already there.

She had repeated to me her father's words, "Fall in love with someone who, when the worst day of your life comes, he is the one you need and want there with you." Her dad's funeral was only a matter of days away, which was surely going to be one of those "worst days" for her, but there was no way I could be that comfort for Summer. I was essentially a stranger to her.

How would that develop over time? She had been open and honest about how she was lonely here in Oregon. Back home she had her friends. Summer didn't need me there like Subi needed me here, so I had no guarantee Summer would ever grow to want me.

I was equally uneasy about the way her life was so intertwined with Z. The only feelings I felt toward him were angry and bitter. Coming into this experiment, I had been fully warned that I was signing up to be a lab rat, but I had deeply underestimated the lengths someone could go to dehumanize another person. Even some of the insane psychology experiments I had read about from the 1950s paled in comparison to what Z had just put me through.

How did he even get away with it? How was it legal? I thought there were all kinds of laws nowadays that kept psychotic psychologists from going too far with their experiments. Clearly the local police knew what was going on. That much was made clear by Officer McKnight, who had approached me during my first week in Oregon, and then again by the look in his eyes at the police station. So, why was Z allowed to put me through such an ordeal? I couldn't help but assume the answer was connected to the way everyone continually told me he had a way of getting people to do things for him. He had connections. He had ways of influencing others.

I wanted nothing more to do with him. I wanted to completely close the short chapter of my life that included Z, and to do so, I would have to also close the chapter on Subi and Summer. It was not an option to have Summer without Z. They may have been on different pages from one another, but they were part of the same book.

"You're just going to go upstairs to pack, aren't you?" Subi asked after stepping out of the truck in the Seaside Hotel parking lot. "And then you're gone."

"Yes. I think I'm ready to go."

"Would it be okay if I come up with you while you pack?"

"Sure. Of course, I don't really have all that much stuff, so it's not like I'm going to be up there very long."

I would have been perfectly happy to be back in my truck within ten minutes and on the road without ever seeing Z's face again, but those plans were dashed as soon as I opened the door to my room. He was standing on my balcony, resting both forearms on the railing and watching something happen down below.

"Miles!" he said, spinning around to look at me with a huge grin. "You got here faster than I was expecting. I was hoping to have this finished before you got home." He waved a hand for me to come join him. When I hesitated, he only waved his hand more vigorously. "Oh, come on. You're gonna love this."

I approached him slowly and peeked over the balcony at the sands below.

There was a machine about the size of a lawnmower slowly rolling around on the sand. It was in its final stages of carving a design. An area about fifty yards square had already been smoothed out and was now being carved up into a swirly design with the name "Lincoln City" featured prominently in the center.

"Isn't it amazing?" Z said. "The prototype arrived today. They did an amazing job. Tim even put racing stripes on the side just for fun. What a nut."

I couldn't possibly care less about this machine. Granted, it was pretty cool, and even this first prototype appeared to be working to perfection, but for whatever reason this actually irritated me more because Z was completely ignoring the obvious elephant in the room.

I wondered for a moment how Z and I could both see the design. This seemed like the type of thing that existed only in the physical world. Then I looked over the railing and saw June in her wheelchair on the grassy area just above the concrete ledge. Everything she saw was updating what Z would see inside his Olinc world.

I turned and walked back into my room without saying a single word. I opened the drawer to my dresser and began pulling out the clothes and putting them on the bed. I had arrived in Lincoln City with only the clothes I was wearing, but I doubted they were going to stop me from taking the nice new clothes I had accumulated over the last handful of months, even if they had all been put on their credit card.

"Oh, come on. Don't be like that," Z said. "We couldn't tell you that any of us were mirror images because we needed to see how you would interact with us."

"You know that's not what he's upset about," Subi said. "Don't talk to him like he's ignorant."

Z turned his attention toward her. "I had very little to do with that. That was between Amos and the local cops."

"The local cops?" I asked. "What about the local cops?"

"They had a bet going on about whether or not Amos could get you to ... you know, push him off the balcony," Z said.

"What were the stakes?" I asked. "How did they even communicate with him?"

"I think Amos owes a steak dinner to about a dozen cops. Maybe more," Z said. "They never spoke to the Amos you know. They have only spoken to the Amos who lives in Idaho."

All of that for a steak dinner. Apparently, that was what my sanity was worth to a handful of cops and to these people who pretended to be my friends. A steak dinner.

"You knew about this?" Subi said to Z. "You're no better than Amos."

"I admit I knew about this, but my focus was different than that of Amos," Z said. He turned his attention back to me. "I needed to see what you were made of, Miles. I needed to know where your loyalty lies. You see, everyone else on the team is technology-minded. I need someone near the top with us who thinks like a consumer, but that someone must be completely loyal. I admit I knew Amos's plan, and I encouraged him to tempt you to stab us in the back. There are going to be a lot of people who are going to try to tempt you along the way to sell them some information, or to completely betray us somehow. We needed to see what you would do in that scenario."

"You're trying to tell me this whole experiment was a job interview for a job I hadn't even applied for?" I mocked. "For a position I didn't even know existed?"

"If you want to be cynical, yes, I guess you could put it that way," Z said. "But I was confident all along that you would be perfect for this team, and that this is the kind of thing you would love to do."

"You sure assume a lot," I said.

Z slapped his hand onto my shoulder. "You see, that's what I like about you. Here I am telling you what you want, and you're not persuaded. I like a man who can think for himself. I loved watching your strength as Amos did his best work on you, and yet, you were a rock."

"Where is Amos, anyway?" I asked.

I didn't exactly feel like giving Amos a hug goodbye, but I couldn't help but be curious where and what he would be doing at a time like this. His whole existence here at the hotel had been centered around experimenting on me, and he lost.

"Amos is gone," Z said. "He unplugged."

"What!?" Subi almost shouted.

"Yeah," Z shrugged his shoulders. "He unplugged even before Miles left the police station. I think he saw no reason for any of this after Miles made it clear he wasn't going to shove him."

"So ... what does that even mean? He unplugged?" I asked even though the main concept of the term seemed obvious.

"Z and I cannot be killed." Subi pointed a finger between the two of them. "If I were to go into my kitchen, grab a long knife, and stab it through Z's heart like he clearly deserves, it would not kill him."

"Hey!" Z protested.

"If we were to get a cut on our hand, we would have to take some time to heal just like you would," Subi continued. "But if we were to fall off a cliff, or get run over by a car, or anything like that ... we would just reset. We would wake up back in our bed in the same shape we had been before the incident."

"Fascinating," I said. "You'll live forever, then? So, where's Amos?"

"We won't live forever," Z said. "We will grow old. Our bodies will fall apart just like everyone else's. We will die of old age. Just like you, we don't know when that will be."

"Only the system knows when we will die," Subi said. "It may be a heart attack or cancer. It could even be Parkinson's disease. Whatever the luck of the draw has in store for us, according to the computations of the system, just like for everyone else. If anything happens to try to take us before that time, we will just wake up in the bed."

"In theory, you mean?" I asked.

"Right. In theory," Subi said. "But it's a pretty good theory."

"As for Amos ... he deleted himself," Z said. "That is the only way one of us can go before dying of old age. It's a pretty simple process. We would just go to our profile on the main computer and ask it to delete us. It'll ask us two or three times if we are sure we want to do that, and when we say we are sure, then ... deleted."

It didn't surprise me that Amos would do something like that. From everything Subi had told me, she considered her existence just as valuable and real as my own. Her own life, if I could call it that, was just as precious as the life of Summer.

Amos, on the other hand, clearly saw little worth in life. He put forth no effort to build himself up. His only goal was to get me to be indifferent toward life as well. He came here with one purpose, and that was to carry out an experiment. Once that experiment was over, he saw no reason to exist.

What a sad way to be.

Thinking about Amos deleting himself changed my entire perspective in an instant. Life was meant to have reason. Life was meant to have purpose. If I were to drive out of this parking lot with the plan of returning to the boring and meaningless life I had before, then what would be the point behind any of it? Was that any better than deleting myself?

Olinc, and whatever limbs could branch off it, had the potential to change lives for the better. It had the potential to change the world. I wanted to be a part of that. As I looked at the face of Z standing there in front of me, I didn't want to let him ruin Olinc.

I was no sucker. I could see right through his façade. He brushed everything off as if everything were Amos's fault, but I knew he was just as much to blame.

I was no sucker. I didn't buy for a second that Amos made this decision to delete himself completely on his own. It was easy to picture Z standing right at Amos's side, urging him—maybe even threatening him in some way—to go through with it.

I wanted to be part of something bigger than myself. This was my chance. I would go back to Idaho, and I would work alongside this horrible man to make this a better world.

I looked over at the beautiful face of Subi standing there close by, and I knew if I were to play my cards right, I wouldn't have to do it alone.

ABOUT THE AUTHOR

Ira Russell has spent a lifetime observing how people adapt to change. After living in thirty different homes across sixteen cities and two countries—including a few years in Central America—he developed a unique fascination with the mechanisms of human behavior and societal survival.

That constant relocation drove him to earn a degree in sociology, followed by seven years working directly with individuals facing profound mental and behavioral challenges. This combination of transient living and deep psychological work fiercely informs his writing. When crafting character-driven speculative fiction, he doesn't just ask "what if"—he applies decades of studying human resilience and fragility to the answer.

A bilingual creator fluent in Spanish, Ira can often be found writing music and performing on stage with his band, crafting leatherwork, or waking up hours before the rest of the world to write. After a lifetime on the move, he has finally dropped anchor in Idaho, where he plans to stay put and build dystopian worlds from the comfort of his own home.

Ira would love to hear from you!

Ira@IraRussell.com

ALSO WRITTEN BY IRA RUSSELL

The Olinc Mirage

He traded a prison cell for a paradise.
He didn't ask what the catch was.

book one: *False Horizon*
book two: *Perfect Reflection*
book three: *Blind Spot*
book four: *Afterimage*

Coming in the fall of 2026...
The Sparks Interference

Three roommates.
One psychic anomaly.
One mystery that will change their frequencies forever.

book one: *Cutting the Static*
book two: *Breaking the Feedback*
book three: *Finding the Resonance*

ONE

A sneak peek at book two of *The Olinc Mirage*

I thought I had fallen in love with a girl, but she wasn't real. She was an artificial intelligence creation, but she wasn't like the AI we all encountered daily. She wasn't programmed to respond any certain way by some team of nerds hiding behind a keyboard somewhere. She wasn't created just to take my lunch order or diagnose my symptoms at the doctor's office.

She was an exact replica of a real person with all her best qualities as well as human imperfections. Her personality was the same. Her appearance was the same. Her voice was the same. Even her touch was the same when she held my hand or kissed me. She was so real, in fact, that I never questioned anything about her. It never crossed my mind that other people couldn't see, feel, or hear her.

I had fallen in love with someone. That much was certain. I obsessed over her. I could not shake her from my mind or my heart. I wanted more than anything to be with her, but the problem was that I didn't know where to direct those feelings. There were two versions of her: one in Oregon who wasn't real, but who cared for me as much as I did for her, and one in Idaho who was as real and tangible as I was, but who barely knew me at all.

By the time I had gotten back to my home in Idaho, I felt silly for having fallen for an AI version of someone. How could I have been so clueless? And yet, I knew there was a real girl out there who was perfect for me, and I couldn't let that fizzle out into nothing.

I didn't want to reach out to her immediately after getting home. Her father had just died, and she had a lot of emotions to sort through along with the funeral arrangements and such. The last thing she needed was some guy she hardly knew coming around trying to spend time with her. So, I waited a week before even considering the idea of reaching out.

After a week had passed, every time I was about to dial her number, I would realize I needed to throw a load of laundry into the machine or wash the dishes or do just about anything but speak to her.

By the time I had been home for two weeks, I no longer needed an excuse to avoid making that call. I had convinced myself that I wasn't as in love with her as I had previously thought. She wasn't real, so my feelings couldn't have been real. I would just move on with my life.

But then Summer called me out of the blue, and my heart immediately felt like it was going to burst out of my chest. Any thoughts of moving on without her, or pretending my love wasn't real, vanished the instant I saw her name on my caller ID.

"Hello there, Miles. Would you be interested in meeting up with me for dinner tonight?"

Hearing her familiar voice was all I needed to rewire my brain.

I stood in front of Epi's Basque Restaurant in Meridian, Idaho, waiting for her to arrive. The restaurant was an old two-story house that had been fixed up and restructured to serve as a quaint destination for culture and dining. A lot of the buildings in this old part of town were like that. Next door was another home from many decades ago that had been fixed up to be a wine bar and restaurant. On the other side of that was what had obviously been a church with tall, vaulted ceilings and large double doors at the front. That church was now a bike shop.

A tiny smart-car-sized cab pulled up to the curb in front of me, and I recognized Summer through the glass. I couldn't help but smile through my nerves. I stepped toward it, but she opened her own door before I could get there. I heard the familiar AI voice over the car's speakers say, "Thank you for choosing Treasure Valley Taxi Services," before she stepped out. Once she closed the door and was next to me on the sidewalk, the empty car waited a few seconds before zipping away.

"It's good to see you again, Miles," Summer said with that familiar smile.

I reached out my hand to offer her a welcoming handshake, but she brushed right past it and wrapped her arms around me for a light hug.

"I can only imagine how weirded out and nervous you must be, but don't worry. I don't bite." She waved at a car as it pulled up to the curb. "I hope it's okay that I invited you to a business dinner. I figured since you and I should probably talk about some things, and since we are going to be working together, this seemed like a good starting point."

"This works out just fine."

"I'm not quite sure how many people we are expecting."

Over the course of the next five minutes, more small cabs pulled up to the curb and people stepped out. They cordially introduced themselves to Summer as they approached. One man and his wife were both dentists. Two other men, who were brothers, owned a dental lab together. A woman in a green pantsuit represented a dental supply company.

Then a large red car pulled up and out stepped a man who *almost* looked familiar to me. I had never seen this man before, but he so closely resembled the appearance of Ramsey that I immediately knew this must be his older brother. He was a few inches taller than Ramsey, and although he was dressed nicely, he didn't appear as though he was trying to make quite the fashion statement his younger brother always made.

I expected his car to pull away just as everyone else's had done, but instead, it rolled only about twenty feet forward to the front of the RESERVED zone and shut down. For a quick moment, I wondered how this would be allowed, but then I remembered the connections and special treatment Ramsey would get everywhere he went.

"Some of you know me, some of you don't," the man said with a wide grin as he greeted our small crowd. "Either way, you are all now my friends. My name is Orson Mir."

Each person in the group echoed in unison the words, "Nice to meet you, Orson."

I caught the eye of Summer as this exchange went on. I could tell by the look in her eye that she was enjoying the introduction. She was relishing the way none of us knew quite what to think of him.

Orson took the lead, and we followed him into the small restaurant. Once inside, the lady at the front desk saw him and then quickly disappeared into a back room. A tiny lady who couldn't have been more than five feet tall came hurrying out to the front lobby, wiping her hands on her apron.

"Orson. Orson," she said with a thick accent, and she placed both hands on his cheeks. "My dear boy, I am so glad you have come to see us. Why did you not tell us you were coming? We would have reserved the upstairs room for you."

"That's okay, Epi. We are happy to take whatever tables you've got," Orson said. "You look pretty busy right now. Is there a long wait? Would it be better for us to come back another day?"

"No. No. Not for my Orson. You get the upstairs room. I know you like the upstairs room. I will give you the upstairs room." Epi patted him on the chest. "I just need a few minutes, okay? Just a few minutes. You wait right here, and I get you the room."

As I looked around, there was not an empty seat in the place. Within a few minutes, another couple stepped into the restaurant, but they were greeted by one of the waiters and informed that they were booked out for the night.

A small group of people soon came down the stairs with take-home containers of their leftovers in hand. Some of them looked frustrated that they were leaving at that moment, while others seemed happy about it. It made me wonder if they had just received their meals for free as they made room for us to take their place.

We ascended the stairs to see Epi wiping down the tables. "Whatever you choose tonight is on the house! My pleasure!" She patted Orson on the cheek again. "Next time, you do not wait so long to come see me again, okay? It has been far too long. Far too long."

Everyone selected a seat and allowed Orson to take his spot at the head of the table. I kept myself glued to Summer's side. I wasn't about to let the group push me into a chair away from her. With all these dental people here, I wasn't the least bit interested in whatever business they were about to do regarding teeth. I was also intrigued by Orson, but I was only here to spend some time with Summer.

"Orson helped rescue Epi's restaurant a few years back," Summer said as she unfolded her napkin and placed it on her lap. "This place was in desperate need of repairs and was about to go under. Orson came here for dinner with some of his friends from the construction world as well as a few other important people, and by the time he went home, they had a plan to gut this place and rebuild."

"It's beautiful," I said as I looked around the room.

Summer took a sip of water from the glass in front of her. "The crew knocked out every wall that wasn't load-bearing. A professional came in to help make some additions and adjustments to the menu. Within a few months, reservations were already booking two weeks out."

"Unless you're Orson. He doesn't seem to need a reservation," I said. "It must have cost him and Ramsey a fortune to get this place back on its feet."

Summer shook her head. "No. That's the thing. Both brothers are very good at getting people to do things. Orson is especially good at bringing people together into a network. It always starts with one person in need, then he finds out who can fill that need, and then he figures out what that second person needs. Before long, he has a whole room full of people scratching each other's backs and everyone involved is glad for it. I don't think Epi had a penny in her bank account when Orson first stepped into her restaurant, but that guy is magic."

"What's in it for him?" I asked. "I mean, that's an awful lot of work for a free meal. What's in it for him?"

"Ramsey and Orson live in a different world than you and I live in. A different world than anyone else in the world. To them, money is just a means to an end. It's the ends that matter," she said. "Ramsey always asks ... 'Who is richer? Is it the guy who has a ton of money and can walk into any restaurant and order off the menu without thinking twice about what it will do to his bank account? Or is the richer guy the one who can walk into any restaurant and not even have to pull out his wallet?'"

"It's an interesting thought," I said.

"A fat cat with a fat wallet could have walked into this restaurant and would have been turned away without a reservation," she said. "But Orson didn't even have to open his mouth, and people were cleared out to make room for him. That's the world they live in around here, and the world they are continuing to expand. It's interesting to watch."

I watched as a waiter brought a stack of menus, but Orson headed him off. Orson took the entire stack from him and skimmed it for only about twenty seconds before informing the waiter, "We will be having the halibut fillet." He handed the stack of menus back to the waiter before addressing everyone at the table. "Did you know that halibut are flounders, but not all flounders are halibut? It's true. They have two eyes, but they are both on the same side of their heads."

Summer raised her hand, "The two of us will have the garlic chicken."

Orson looked at her incredulously. "I think you want the halibut."

"No, Orson," Summer said. "Halibut is not what we want. Tonight, we want the chicken."

Orson stared at her for a long, awkward moment. He didn't look angry. Rather, her choice seemed to leave him more confused. I couldn't tell if he was mystified that she wanted something different from what he had chosen for us, or if he was baffled at the way she was standing up to him.

"Last time we came you had the halibut, and you loved it," Orson said. "I distinctly remember you saying it was perhaps the best fish you'd ever had."

"That's true," she said. "I do love their halibut, but—"

"Halibut for everyone it is, then." Orson cut her off.

"No. Tonight I am having the garlic chicken, and so is Miles," she said matter-of-factly.

Orson continued to stare at her, but she was no longer looking at him. She held her glass of water up to her lips and took another sip as the entire room looked back and forth between them as if they were watching a tennis match. Orson eventually waved his hand at the waiter without saying a word, which left me clueless as to who had just won the battle over menu items.

"Don't worry," Summer whispered to me after the waiter disappeared once again down the stairs. "You and I will be eating the chicken tonight."

"I'm so relieved. I just can't do fish. It's the worst."

"I know. You're not that hard to read. I could see it all over your face the second he mentioned the whole table was getting the halibut. I really do love the halibut, but I know it's not for everyone."

"You didn't want me to be the only one to get something different." I moved around some of the utensils in front of me. "You sacrificed what you wanted for what you assumed I wanted."

"It wasn't a difficult assumption." She smiled. "Like I said, you're not all that hard to read. And I gambled on the fact that pretty much everyone likes chicken."

"What if I were a vegetarian?"

"I doubt that." She shook her head. "That seems like the kind of thing that would have come up in conversation with Subi somewhere along the line."

"Do you talk to Subi often?"

"Yes. Pretty often. At least once a week."

I had to wonder what that would be like. Subi was what they called a "mirror image" of herself. Using the microchip implanted in Summer's brain, the company collected all kinds of data regarding her emotions, actions, and sensations. Whether it be fear, love, frustration ... every bit of experience she had would feed into the system. As it did so, this mirror image of Summer would update in real time. Having a conversation with that mirror image, whom I had always known as Subi, was just like having a conversation with Summer herself.

As I sat there slicing off pieces of garlic chicken, and as I tuned out the conversations and negotiations regarding dental work going on around me, I couldn't help but ask myself what types of conversations I would have with a mirror image of myself. It wouldn't be quite like having a friend listen to me. If I were to hold something back from a friend, they would be none the wiser. I would never be able to do that in conversation with a copy of myself because my mirror image would see right through any intentional self-deception.

Over the past few weeks, I had tried to convince myself that Summer didn't want or need me around, or that I didn't need or want her either. If I'd had another version of myself with whom I could literally have a conversation—one that completely and utterly wanted the best for me just as I did—then that form of me would have shut down those lies I had been telling myself. It would have been an interesting tool to have at my disposal as I sorted myself out.

Although not everyone around the table was happy about getting fish for dinner and there was a lot of food left on some of the plates, it was easy to see that everyone left the meal feeling like they had accomplished something positive. Everyone seemed to feel like they were getting the best part of the deal. This man would be doing a favor for that guy, and that guy for that lady, and so on all around the group. There were also names being tossed around regarding people who had already given a handshake deal regarding some part of the process, and even a few names of people who Orson was sure would be on board once they were brought up to speed.

I couldn't help but wonder what would happen if someone didn't live up to their end of the bargain. There were a lot of cogs in these wheels. If one of them wasn't spinning properly, the entire system would be thrown out of whack.

As people began to stand up from the table and shake hands, I lifted the napkin from my lap and wiped the corners of my mouth before laying it on the table next to my plate. I pushed my chair back and was about to stand up when Summer reached over and grabbed my hand.

"Hold up for a minute," she said. "I'd like to talk to you."

I looked down at her left hand, which was still on top of mine. As had been the case the few other times I had seen Summer in person, she still wore a modest wedding ring on that hand. This was one thing that was different between Summer and her mirror image, Subi. Subi never wore the wedding ring, but Summer kept it on because she had a hard time letting go of her failed marriage, even though the divorce had been finalized years ago.

"My life is not as simple as you think it is," Summer said once the room had cleared out and we were alone. "The girl you knew in Oregon is an awful lot like me, but we are not the same."

"I'm hoping you'll give me a chance to decide that for myself. You just need a chance to get to know me. At least, I'm hoping you will give me that chance."

She pulled her hand back and folded her hands into her lap. She looked me over for a long moment before finally saying, "There are a lot of things about my life you don't understand. If I were to just tell you nothing is going to happen between you and me, then that would only leave you upset and confused. I can see that. And I can see that it's my own fault—well, Subi's fault, which is my own fault, sort of."

Although I didn't like where this conversation was going, I couldn't help but grin at the uniqueness of her reasoning.

She sighed. "I can tell you won't understand unless I let you into my life a little. My real life, that is. I owe you that much." She stood up from the table and laid her napkin next to her plate. "Let's go to my house."

MAILING LIST
(I WILL NEVER SPAM YOU)

The main focus of the email list is to keep readers up to date on new released, but every once in a blue moon I will include a short, true story from my past about a pickle I got myself into—like the time my buddies and I ran away from Boy Scouts camp to go hunting for Bigfoot, or the time I walked into the wrong hotel room when on the road with my baseball team.

Just enter your email into the website. That's it!

IraRussell.com

Ira@IraRussell.com

www.ingramcontent.com/pod-product-compliance
Lightning Source LLC
LaVergne TN
LVHW091140080826
845145LV00008B/2205